NOT OTHERWISE SPECIFIED

Also by Hannah Moskowitz

Break

Invincible Summer

Gone, Gone, Gone

Teeth

NOT OTHERWISE SPECIFIED

HANNAH MOSKOWITZ

Simon Pulse

NEW YORK   LONDON   TORONTO   SYDNEY   NEW DELHI

SIMON PULSE

An imprint of Simon & Schuster Children's Publishing Division

1230 Avenue of the Americas, New York, NY 10020

This Simon Pulse edition March 2015

Text copyright © 2015 by Hannah Moskowitz

Cover photograph of girl copyright © 2015 by Jill Wachter

Cover photograph of pool table copyright © 2015 by Jasper James/Millennium Images

Cover photo-illustration copyright © 2015 by David Field

All rights reserved, including the right of reproduction in whole or in part in any form.

SIMON PULSE and colophon are registered trademarks of Simon & Schuster, Inc.

For information about special discounts for bulk purchases,

please contact Simon & Schuster Special Sales at 1-866-506-1949

or business@simonandschuster.com.

The Simon & Schuster Speakers Bureau can bring authors to your live event. For more information or to book an event, contact the Simon & Schuster Speakers Bureau at 1-866-248-3049 or visit our website at www.simonspeakers.com.

Cover designed by Karina Granda

Interior designed by Hilary Zarycky

The text of this book was set in Electra LT Std.

Manufactured in the United States of America

2 4 6 8 10 9 7 5 3

The Library of Congress has cataloged the hardcover edition as follows:

Moskowitz, Hannah.

Not otherwise specified / Hannah Moskowitz. — First Simon Pulse hardcover edition.

p. cm.

Summary: Auditioning for a New York City performing arts high school could help Etta escape from her Nebraska all-girls school, where she is not gay enough for her former friends, not sick enough for her eating disorders group, and not thin enough for ballet, but it may also mean real friendships.

[1. Interpersonal relations—Fiction. 2. Bisexuality—Fiction. 3. Performing arts—Fiction. 4. Bullying—Fiction. 5. Eating disorders—Fiction. 6. African Americans—Fiction. 7. Nebraska—Fiction.] I. Title.

PZ7.M84947Not 2015   [Fic]–dc23   2014011032

ISBN 978-1-4814-0596-6 (hc)

ISBN 978-1-4814-0595-9 (pbk)

ISBN 978-1-4814-0598-0 (eBook)

To Kat and Katie:
my girls

NOT OTHERWISE SPECIFIED

1

TIME FOR THE ETTA-GETS-HER-GROOVE-BACK PARTY. IT WOULD BE easier if I'd been invited, or if this party actually existed, but whatever. I made my entire Halloween costume this year from a bag of sequins and a turtleneck. I can make things work.

Except right now even that enormous bedazzled turtleneck wouldn't fit me, because I broke up with Ben the week before Christmas and started eating disorder treatment a few weeks before that. (*Cut out toxic influences!* my counselor said, and I'm still trying to figure out if *Dump the boyfriend who weighs less than you!* was a completely rational application of that, but whatever. I didn't love him and he didn't love me so minimal harm minimal foul.) And apparently those two things added up to an entire winter break of me on the couch eating jugs of ice cream off a wooden spoon because a regular spoon wasn't big enough for the scoops I wanted to shovel down my throat. Stay classy, Ett.

I'm not freaking out about it. I'm really not going to go down that road. Recovery was my choice, and sometimes it sucks like I can't believe, but the truth is I am really damn positive about it and yeah, I'm not under any delusion that ice cream binges are the key to a happy relationship with food, but it's better than not eating at all. Except for the simple and really unemotional fact that I'm going to the judgmental hot zone that is a gay club tonight and none of my clothes fit.

"Kristina!" I'm halfway out of this halter top that wouldn't even go past my boobs. I was about one-third boob *before* recovery (I was never one of those pretty little stick thing anorexics; I was a chubby black girl who never quite hit not-chubby), and now I'm quickly closing in on one-half.

"What?" Kristina is fifteen and gorgeous.

I finally wrestle the halter off and onto the floor. "Do you have anything I can wear?"

Her eyebrows come together. "You're going out?" I haven't been out of sweatpants in three weeks. Can't exactly blame her.

"The Dykes are at Cupcake tonight. I'm gonna meet up."

"You guys are talking again?" I don't know if I ever really told Kristina about our falling-out or if she just heard about it at school before break started. We both go to Saint Emily's Preparatory Academy for Young Women. It's a small school because who the hell would ever want to go to Saint Emily's Preparatory Academy for Young Women, so news travels fast.

"Not exactly. They're all over Facebook posting what they're wearing. I'm just gonna show up and be all contrite."

"Suck face with some chicks to get back in their good favor?"

"Ding ding ding. Do you have anything?"

She thinks and says, "Yeah. Hang on," and comes back with a red dress that is so completely Year Eight, Kristina, my dear. I try it on anyway, but even my boobs can't make this sexy.

I say, "Anything, uh . . ."

"Sluttier?"

"The best little sister."

"Yeah, come on." She brings me to her room, and I root through her closet until I find this tight black skirt that I think will fit, bless my baby girl's hips, and this pink shirt that says "BITCH" on it in jewels.

"Uh. Later we're going to be talking about why you have these."

"Halloween."

"What were you for Halloween?"

"You."

". . . Right."

"Have fun."

●　●　●

Nebraska—all of Nebraska—has one thing going for it, one tiny pink little light in the middle of its giant mass of cornfield and suck, and it's Club Cupcake, the grossest, most run-down piece of shit you can imagine. Big Xs behind the windows so you can't see in, no name on the front, just this tacky-ass Christmas-light cupcake. I don't even know if Cupcake is its real name. But for the past two years—since I started high school, since I got my fake ID, since I found this place where I actually *belong*—this place has been the sparkly little Barbie Dreamhouse we always wanted, filled with plastic guys and glitter, but with bonus sticky floors and girls who lick other girls. This place was our freaking castle.

Cupcake is (a) sketchy, and (b) the only gay bar in Schuyler, Nebraska (best known for its beef-processing plant—how I wish that were some sort of sexual euphemism), so therefore it is (c) packed. I'm all of five-foot-nothing, so finding the Dykes is going to be a feat, even though we always stand out. We're called the Disco Dykes for a reason; we're very throwback, hot pants and tie-dye, very vehemently seventies because when you're five lesbians at an all-girls school, you have to be very vehemently *something* or else you start thinking about how everyone thinks you're a sexual predator. Or, worse, you start thinking, *the horrible beasts in this school are what girls are*, these are the reason you had to come out to your parents and you have to put up with every other politician hating your guts. You did that because you apparently want to sleep with *these girls*, when the reality is that most times you want to push these girls down the stairs. (And *bi* the way, I was never a lesbian, and I told the Dykes that all the time, but there isn't a Banjo Bisexuals group or whatever and anyway, Rachel and I were best friends since preschool, so it wasn't as if I was going to turn down a group that gave me a chance to hang with her, to dance with her, to make out with her, and as long as I dated girls and shut up about boys it was never a problem.) The Disco Dykes are a Saint Em's tradition. They've been around since it was founded. In the eighties. It's like the most screwed-up little sorority for high schoolers. It's so stupid, except it was totally my life.

I didn't realize Ben would be some big political move. What's ridiculous is that it's not like I started dating a lacrosse-playing Young Republican. Ben was straight in name only, really, because I met him at a gay club and he did volunteer work with Pride Alliance, and aside from his ugly shoes and his weird hair and the way he'd slam me into walls and breathe on my neck, there wasn't much straight about him. I actually met him here. He was with some gay friends of his, he was cute, it wasn't a big deal—until I turned around and the Dykes had abandoned me there and I got to school the next day and they wouldn't talk to me. I'm so incredibly far from defending their shitty behavior, but the truth is that second semester of junior year starts tomorrow, and I want some friends, damn it, and all-girls school is bad enough when you *do* have a pack.

Plus, you know. Rachel.

It makes us sound like we're some cult, how I'm not allowed to date guys, but it really isn't like that. We were people who were brought together by a common interest called making out with girls, but it's not like we put up flyers, you know? We had to find each other. We had to be interested in each other. What I'm saying is that we had to look at each other.

We picked out earrings together. I had dinner at Isabel's house. I cried on Titania's lap during horror movies. I was Rachel's whole world.

It would be so much easier if I hadn't loved them.

No, it would be so much easier if they hadn't loved me.

Except I can fix this. I'm back and better than ever, and since Ben and I never got to Facebook-official which means the Dykes have no way of knowing that we broke up, I'll tell them and everything will back to normal. I drink vodka from the water bottle I snuck in because my says-I'm-twenty ID is good but my says-I'm-twenty-two ID is a waste-of-fifteen-dollars piece of shit, plus Cupcake's just beer and wine anyway, and I'm not looking for something to sip. Pure liquid courage, thanks. I can't believe I'm scared of these girls. They used to be my friends.

They are my friends. I'll tell them Ben and I broke up, we'll laugh about it, I'll say I'll never do it again and whatever maybe I won't, maybe I'll just stick with girls until college (until New York, until big city, until *not Nebraska*). That's doable. It's not *reasonable*, but that's why I'm drinking.

I've circled almost the entire place and collided with almost ten glitter-doused gay boys before I see them. They're perched on a cluster of armchairs tucked in by the bar. Natasha's wearing rhinestone hot pants and a hat that I am not entirely sure is seventies, actually, Isabel's in flares and sunglasses because Isabel is the biggest stereotype imaginable, and Titania's in this tie-dye maxi dress that I have to admit I would kill for. They wear this shit all the time, but I only ever did it when I was with them. We keep this stuff in our lockers so we can change out of our uniforms right after school, and when I started dating Ben they broke into my locker and stole all my clothes. It would be funny if it weren't ruining my life.

Okay, it's still kind of funny.

Rachel's not here.

Maybe that'll make this easier. They very obviously do not look up when I come over.

"Hey." I offer the water bottle to Natasha because she (it used to be me) is the ringleader if Rachel isn't here and I should probably follow the pecking order since these girls have lately shown that they have the manners of wild animals. She takes it and stares at me while she drinks. This is either a good sign or a waste of vodka.

"Where's Rachel?" I ask.

No answer.

"Guys?"

"Babysitting," Isabel says, like I'm so stupid, like they've told me this a billion times and why wasn't I listening. At least it's probably true. Rachel has twin three-year-old sisters.

"Anyone good here tonight?" I say.

Natasha hands the bottle back. My hand is shaking. Christ.

"I like her," I say, pointing to who-the-hell-cares. "I like fishnets. Reminds me of ham or something I can eat." This is an old standby, these self-deprecating chubby-girl jokes, and I'm nervous as hell and I guess I'm falling back on old habits. Next thing you know I'll be in the bathroom gagging up three hundred calories of vodka. (I will not be, do I look like a pushover?)

(Okay, maybe right now, shaking in front of my ex-best friends, maybe right now I do.)

Isabel says, "Something you can eat? You mean like a penis?" and Titania giggles.

"Cute," I say. "Can I sit?"

Natasha says, "What are you even doing here, Etta?"

Stalking you. "What are you talking about?"

"This is a gay club."

"You're not really serious with this gay-exile thing, right? Jesus, I get it, you were mad." You were stupid and out of line to be mad, but I leave that part out. "This isn't really going to be a big deal, right? Hey, Ben and I broke up. We can pretend it never happened if it'll make you guys feel better."

"It's not about us *feeling better*."

"You're actually serious."

The music picks up, and Natasha raises her voice. It's really hard to convince myself that she isn't yelling at me. "This is hard enough as it is, and then you have to go and completely piss on everything we stand for. Did you miss the part where the heteros make our life shit? And now here you are slutting around with the first guy who's nice to you, and what do you think that does besides make us all look like we're just doing this lesbian thing for attention? I get enough of that bullshit from my brothers, thanks."

"Do your brothers happen to mention how really mature you are?"

"Screw you."

"Whatever. I'll call Rachel later. We broke *up*, Tasha."

"Yeah, well, the world's full of boys."

"Warn Rachel to change her number if you want."

"Yeah, I'll do that."

Flawless comeback, Tasha.

"And by the way?" she shouts after me. And this time I think she is yelling at me. "'Bitch' is sexist gendered language and I'm pretty disgusted you decided to wear it right over your tits. And by the way?" She pauses there.

I can't stand it. I turn around. "By the way what?"

"By the way," she says. She's smiling. "You always were a little bitch."

2

TODAY IS OUR FIRST DAY BACK AT SCHOOL, BUT IT'S ON A TUESDAY, weirdly, which means I have my six a.m. tap class before school. It's a ridiculous time to be dancing, but until Dyke-pocalypse, my after-school time was taken up by Pride Alliance and by chorus, which I still have, and my eating disorder support group, which is new and wouldn't have fit into my old schedule anyway, back when I did ballet. But I don't do ballet anymore.

I like to be in the back for tap class, not because I don't want to be looked at, not because I'm shy, not even because I don't want to see myself in the mirror, but just because I like to be in my own place when I dance. The other girls in my class are giggly and chatty between exercises, laughing at each other when they mess up and whispering about people from the public school everyone goes to but me. It's not that I don't like them, or that I'm not friendly with them, because I am. I'm friendly with them after class or on break, but when I'm dancing, I want it to be just me. I do chorus to get out there and interact with people. I did Pride for the same reason. Hell, I do ED group for the same reason. Even though tap has never been my favorite, it, you know, fills the void. I did tap as a little kid but picked it back up a few years ago because my ex-girlfriend was into it, and I never gave it up out of spite, because it wasn't that kind of breakup.

It's not hard to be in my own world today, because I'm busy having some inner-monologue freakout about what happened at Cupcake last night, not to mention the really stressful conversation with my mother this morning about why she hasn't seen the Dykes lately. (She didn't call them "the Dykes," just like she won't say "eating disorder" out loud. She'll throw in a *Um, so, how's group?* every once in a while to prove she's rooting for me without actually having to do anything, and I think treatment is convincing me I have deep-seated issues with my mom, or hell, maybe I actually do, because it's not like she's ever said "bisexual" out loud either.) Even everyone in dance class clacking together, this sound I always love, isn't pulling me out of this.

I make more mistakes than usual, and when Ms. Hoole calls me over at the end of class, I'm completely prepared to be chewed out. She likes me, because to be perfectly honest

I could dance these other girls under a table, but that also means she expects all these things from me, and if there's one thing I've been trying to convince people since the time I was freaking born and have completely failed to get through to people is not to expect things from me, but guess what happens when you're a rich black was-ballerina in *Nebraska*, you know? I mean, excuse me for wanting to make out with girls instead of guys under all that pressure, you know?

But she doesn't chew me out. She says, "This came into the office and I thought of you right away. You're always talking about New York."

Of course I'm always talking about New York. New York is the theater kid's Jerusalem. When I was seven, I had four different stuffed animals all named Manhattan, and one enormous plush frog named Juilliard.

I take the flyer.

"One of the best arts high schools in the whole country," she says, like I'm new. "Holding auditions for a few more scholarship students for next year."

I've applied to Brentwood every semester since I was a freshman. My mom fought me on it at first, but I think at this point she's resigned herself to the fact that I'm never going to get in, so she just signs the forms without arguing. I mean, it's *Brentwood*, so to get accepted you not only have to dance like you're in *Black Swan* and belt out a B over high C like it's a middle G and cry on cue through a memorized six thousand lines of Shakespeare, but you have to do it all at once, while having a 4.0 and forking over a hundred thousand dollars and giving the admissions director a blow job, apparently, but once you're in, you're in, it's Brentwood then Juilliard then fame and fortune, and even if not, it's New York City, baby, and the most important part of this equation is Brooklyn Bridge at midnight and tiny dogs in Chelsea and the Staten Island Ferry and that ex-girlfriend (don't think about that, should I think about that?) and the answer to the goddamn equation is the absolute value of *not Nebraska*.

"I've never even been called for an audition," I say. "I think they just shred my applications on sight by now. 'Etta again?' *Zzzzt*."

"This is different," she says. "Read the damn flyer! Talent search. Starts with the audition and all the paperwork comes after. I have a friend who works there, and she's implied that they've been getting a lot of applications from overinflated entitled egos delicate-flowering around the place."

"So they're starting with the auditions?"

"Maybe they want to see people in person before they can be dazzled by the credentials. Meet someone who sparkles in person, not just on paper."

"Someone like me?"

"Yeah, kiddo. Someone like you." She hands me another piece of paper. "And this, m'dear, is a group of kids getting together to practice for the auditions together. Maybe make some friends, get some practice in?" It's in the same community center as my chorus and my ED group, meeting just a little while after ED.

The thing is that it feels like a sign.

The thing is the Brooklyn Bridge at midnight and tiny dogs in Chelsea and the Staten Island Ferry.

And the thing is that she just called me sparkly, and the last time anyone even hinted that I was sparkly, I was at Cupcake making out with a girl and covered in actual glitter. And now I'm standing here just sweaty and too-tight-leotarded, just me.

I change into my uniform—what up, Mary Janes, missed you not—in the car and mess my dreads up because the last thing you want to be is too pretty when you're a (not) lesbian at an all-girls school. I definitely need to look like I'm not trying to pick anyone up. Uglying-down is an old habit at this point, but it's the first day back and it feels weird. Maybe because this is the first time I'm doing it by myself instead of half-naked in the backseat of Natasha's car while we draw on messy eyeliner and change out of the disco clothes we wore only for the drive to school, just on principle. I smudge my lipstick.

Saint Em's is very old-British-boarding-school style, except it's not an old castle, just some thirty-year-old building trying to look like an old castle in the middle of nowhere, but the first thing you see when you walk in are those bright-green metal lockers, so, very subtle, school. Plus girls are gross and rich girls are worse so it's kind of a vandalized mess.

If it isn't obvious, I hate it here.

I open my locker and well, awesome, that's interesting. There are condoms filled with what-the-hell-even-is-that hanging off the hooks inside my locker, the hooks where I used to hang my aforementionedly-stolen disco clothes. I really need to change my combination.

I wonder which of them deigned to buy condoms. They probably found some guy to do it. God forbid anyone in the world ever think they're straight. (Or bisexual, I don't know if you've heard of this? It's a thing!)

God. It's just that I really thought stuff was going to go back to normal.

One of the condoms is dripping onto my history textbook. Whatever. I give in and taste it. Ranch dressing. All right then.

At lunch I make sure they're looking at me at my new loner loser table (Rachel's not there; I overheard her bio partner saying she has strep throat), and I squeeze a condom right on top of my salad. Titania makes this big show of gagging.

"Fat dyke," this junior bitch Liliana mumbles as she glides past my table, and I ignore her, because yeah right, pay more attention, Liliana. She slips past me, and I focus again on the Dykes.

I dip my finger into the condom and lick it clean. 148 calories and my daily value of *screw you*. Delicious.

3

GROUP.

We sit in a circle in flimsy desks, about exactly how these things are set up on TV, except crazy people on TV have this habit of not actually being crazy, because actual screwed-up people aren't cuddly and relatable. We're too busy leaning back in our seats so that our stomachs won't touch the desk, and jiggling our knees and tapping our feet because any movement is better than nothing and body checking, fingers around wrists, thumbs on the sides of waists, our fingers knitted together, squeezing, our nails tapping against collarbones. Then there are the girls who won't even sit down—who *can't* sit down, because standing burns more calories and shuffling their feet really burns more calories, and maybe they want us to feel like they're better than us, or maybe they don't, or maybe they are just so, so past giving a shit what people think about them. We're all here because it's not fun for us anymore, but those are the girls who make you realize that this shit hasn't been fun for a really, really long time. They're shifting, shivering statues, and *this is what you wanted to be. At some point there really was a choice.* At some point you really did jump off a cliff, and we can sit here and cry about it all we want about how *no*, we were not expecting what would be at the bottom, and we just wanted to be skinny and we just wanted to disappear and be perfect and be noticed and to be in control and to starve and purge out everything that's wrong with us, but at some point we decided we were going to do this and the thing is that you *don't* disappear (and that's really it, isn't it), you linger around and wilt in the corners of community rec centers.

I'm one of the bigger girls here, but there are actually a bunch around my size. One of them's Taylor, who's talking right now about how frustrating this whole diagnostic process is. You have to have a BMI under a certain ridiculous number *and* you have to stop getting your period to be diagnosed anorexic, so that rules out me and the two boys I sometimes forget are here. The diagnoses are something we've talked about a billion times, and it's something our leader *still* lets us talk about because it's still goddamn frustrating.

"I just want that stupid label," Taylor says. Taylor doesn't curse. Taylor says "stupid." "And it's ridiculous because, like, the whole *issue* at school is *stop labeling me, stop putting me in your stupid box*, and then here I am dying to count as anorexic instead of 'eating disordered not otherwise specified.'"

"My doctor wouldn't even say that out loud," I say. "Like, I've read the DSM entries, I know it's EDNOS, but she just says 'It's not the diagnosis that's important.'"

"But that is important to you," says Angela, our leader. She's older than we are and licensed or something.

"There are a billion things about this that are important to me and every one of them contradicts or takes away from one of the other ones. I just want this to add up in a way that makes me look more . . ."

"Sane?" Angela tries.

"Legitimate," says a voice, tiny, in the corner. I don't even have to look up to know who it is, because even though she doesn't talk very much, when she does, it's in that broken, significant voice. If this were a movie, everyone would part around her, but instead it's just a little shifting around and a few turned heads. You still can't see her. She stands in the back—I've never seen her sit down—and she is the smallest of the small. Blonder than blond but not bleached, I don't think, too muted and wispy to be intentional. Just natural, a little dull. A lot of the skinny girls are toothpicks. Bianca is smoke.

I have this fascination with her because she's young— fourteen—which is one of the few things she's ever said about herself, and because I can tell by her clothes that she's poor, and because she just looks so sick and so sad. She's the

Tiny Tim of our group, and a part of me maybe doesn't believe she's real. She's just *too* tragic. She's the shattered little girl at the beginning of the fairy tale, and I can't shake this feeling that if she would just get better then we all would. But I also feel so sure that she is never, ever going to be okay. Maybe the fascination is that I'm kind of waiting for her to die. I'd feel worse about this if I didn't know from experience that she's waiting for it too.

Taylor talks some more, but I feel drained and done for the day. I wish I were at chorus instead, which is weird for me because I've never been a huge fan of chorus. I don't even know why I do it, except that it felt weird to be such a ridiculous musical theater geek but not be in any singing group. How am I going to pretend my life is a Special Musical Episode if I never sing? How am I going to even pretend I'm qualified for a musical theater audition if I sit at home and watch *Cabaret* over and over and don't at least try to sing? So I get out, I try, I sing.

The thing is that I'm not that good. I don't know. This whole audition process just sounds like something they'd do in that episode of whatever that show was when they're supposed to attempt something they'd fail at, and everyone fails as expected and ends up hating themselves. It feels about that likely that I'm going to get into Brentwood or even get past the first round of auditions, and do I really need to hate myself right now? I have four angry lesbians handling that job pretty well.

Well, three. I still have no proof Rachel hasn't forgiven me. I tried calling her last night but she didn't pick up. Babysitting, I guess. Or strep. Maybe her sisters have strep too, that would keep her busy. Probably that.

Group ends, and yeah, maybe I creepily watch Bianca a little when she's packing up, but actually that's because I want to leave when she's leaving because she has this ridiculously hot older brother—I thought maybe it was her boyfriend at first, but she actually brings it up all the time, *my brother's picking me up today*, all this warmth in her voice, she loves him—who comes and gets her sometimes, and seeing him is depressingly often the highlight of my week, and it will definitely make me feel better about the fact that I've been sitting here studying his little sister's non-body for an hour with some mixture of jealousy or lust and Jesus Christ Etta she is fourteen and *sick*, this is not sexy. And it's not even that I think it is, or that when I close my eyes to dream about girls, I see ones who look anything like her. It's just that I can't ever get out of my head what it would feel to touch a body like that. And, you know. For a variety of reasons I'm never going to get there. The biggest one being that I really do mostly not want to.

I really hate group. I really do.

Bianca slips her backpack over her shoulder—she has this really deliberate way of moving, and I wonder if she does ballet, figures that she would, really, but I know most of the advanced girls in the state and it's not like I'd forget her—so I fiddle with my coat for a while to look natural and then I leave too. Her brother drives this shabby car and never gets out, but seriously, I just want to glance at his face and walk home writing a little song to myself about how he obviously noticed me and fell in love with me and we're going to have beautiful children and raise them to be happier than his sister, or me.

Except I am happy, most of the time. That's the messed-up part of this.

Even with all of this, I'm just a happy damn person. I lie around watching scary movies with my sister and knitting with my mom and I tap dance and I ace math tests and I am happy.

It could just be a lot easier to be happier right now, is the thing.

Bianca doesn't head outside, which means no hope of seeing Hot Brother today. Poor me. She's heading somewhere else inside the building, so I give up and look at this flyer to find the audition group, and the flyer has little drawings of musical notes on it and I get so stupidly excited. I headbang to some imaginary music and hop up the stairs.

I will pass by the third floor without looking in. I will pass by the third floor without looking in. Damn it, this is why I am not supposed to stick around the community center after group. Go straight home, go cry into a bowl of fruit, don't think.

I keep winding up another set of stairs and then down a hallway, and it gets harder and harder to ignore that Bianca's headed in the same direction. I start to feel really awkward about it and duck into the bathroom for a minute. It gives me some time to tug and tug on this shirt I'm wearing, this old, pre-Dyke T-shirt I found balled up on the floor of my closet because I obviously wasn't going to wear my uniform to group, but my seventies clothes don't fit well and to be honest I was a little happy about that because I really, really did not want to wear them. Not anymore.

It's not like I ever looked good in hot pants anyway.

Because seriously, no one looks good in hot pants.

I get to the audition room and don't see Bianca, so maybe she was headed to something different after all. Or maybe she's itsy-bitsy and standing behind a normal-size person. Honestly I don't spend a lot of time thinking about it, because my headbanging and all my thoughts are swallowed up by this tiny room overflowing with actual music. There's a piano, but no one's really playing it. People are every once in a while just wandering over to play a few notes, check pitch, and I can't hear it anyway over the twenty people singing on top of each other. It's not pretty. Everyone's singing and reciting monologues, alone or in small groups. Two people are singing "On My Own," and only one is on key. Everyone has their fingers pressed into the insides of their ears so they can hear the sound reverberating off their jawbone. Trick of the trade, and it makes the loud room bearable.

Makes it kind of amazing.

Chorus is fine, but it's a lot of nineteenth-century chamber music, and I am not nineteenth-century chamber music. I'm "Out Tonight" and "No Good Deed" and "Let's Hear It for the Boy," the last of which I'm hearing right now from somewhere in the corner, ringing out through everything. It's one of those voices I've always been jealous of, one that's so clear and clean and sounds so *effortless*, like whoever it is is just opening their mouth and the words are falling out, like she doesn't even need to breathe.

So I look and . . . well.

It's Bianca.

And that guy sitting next to her, coaching her gently? That'd be Hot Brother.

So, you know, that's a thing. I'm going to be sticking around, I think. (What the hell else am I going to do, go home and wait for Rachel to not call?)

I sing and talk to people and tell them they're awesome and they tell me I'm awesome back, and I mean it for a few of them and maybe a few of them even mean it for me, and eventually people start clearing out. The first round of auditions aren't until next week, so I guess I don't know how this works. No one made any announcements. Mostly I just sang and didn't think, and it was surprisingly . . . nice. It was just nice.

But maybe Bianca can tell me what we're really doing here, so I give her this little smile across the room, and when most people are gone I go to her and say, "You are really, really good."

Bianca jumps like I touched her, or like I hit her, even.

"Shit, sorry. I'm Etta," I say. "I'm in group with you."

"I know," she says, but she doesn't say it mean. She says it like she's *ashamed* that I approached her first, like she thinks she's *let me down*, and maybe that's a lot for me to get from two words, or maybe it's just hitting a little too close to home. (What self-starved girl isn't letting *everyone* down? Seriously.)

Because, really, I don't think anyone who's ever been within two miles of Bianca would expect her to be the type to make the first move.

Here I am thinking like I know her. I get like this with girls. I just do. (Rachel said it was one of her favorite things about me. Rachel said, *You care so much, Etta, you care so much about getting your ass laid, that's what this really is, huh, go get 'em tigress.*)

(This isn't that. This is *let me see your scars, let me show you mine too.*)

(This is maybe a little *how the hell did you get this thin.*)

So instead I say, "You do a damn good job with a song meant for a big black girl."

"Those are the best songs."

"I'm gonna tell my mom that. She thinks all girls should be Kristin Chenoweth."

"Did you know that her real name is Kristi?"

I say, "It is?"

Bianca and I are the same height, I realize. That doesn't happen much. "Chenoweth," she says. "Her real name is Kristi. She added the *n* to look more serious."

"No way."

Jesus, *gently*, Etta. She looks like she's worried I'm going to shove her at a polygraph. "Um, yes," she says. "Sorry. I should go." I'm watching her gather up her stuff, watching those skinny damn arms—Jesus Christ—when I see a hand come down onto her shoulder. Well hey there, Hot Brother.

"Hi," I say. "I'm Etta."

"James. Hey."

"My sister's name is Kristina," I say to Bianca. "I'll tell her to chop the *a* off. She wants to be a librarian, so serious is probably better."

Bianca smiles a little and looks up at James. "Etta's my friend from . . ." She looks at me like she thinks I might not want it said. Aw, sweetie.

But then for some reason I can't say it. He picks her up every week, she's about to break in half, seriously, this is not a secret. And I don't mind people knowing, not now that I'm getting better. It kind of helps to talk about it, to hear people say their stupid little things about how they're proud of me, because yeah, you know what, I started therapy because I felt like it and not because I got forced into it like practically every other girl in my group. I'm proud of me too, y'know?

So screw it. "We're in that eating-disorder group together," I say.

He says, "Hey, see, Bee? I knew there were cool girls in there." He smiles at me. "She tries to tell me none of the girls in there have any interests other than . . ."

"Sticking their fingers down their throats?" I say.

"Oh, yes, we like her," James says. "Etta can stay."

"I'm a big proponent of no-fingers-down-throat," I say. "I should have a shirt made up."

"Etta's good," Bianca says, quietly. "Etta's always saying brave things. Inspiring."

"Damn, girl. Thank you." I can't think of any inspiring thing I've said, but I guess I do say stuff that's a lot lighter than some of the girls, and that when it gets too heavy I'm always inclined to be like *hey so how about this puppy I saw this weekend!!* and pass my phone around. It's a defense mechanism, whatever, but so's half the shit people do, and at least being kind of irreverent makes me happy, and here's this girl calling it brave and inspiring, so that's pretty badass. Really it's hard to be in that group and not feel like I just think *differently* from these girls, that everything's a little sparklier for me than it is for them. Sometimes this shit just isn't so bad. I mean yeah, recovery sucks, my friends dumped me, I've just been way outshined by a room full of singers, but it could be all that and also raining, you know?

James says, "We're actually going out to get some food

now. There's a local co-op place she likes. Do you want to come? No stress."

I look at her. "Would that be okay?"

She nods.

"Yeah, I'd like that a lot." Human interaction!

"Awesome," James says. "Mason's coming too. Mason!"

A guy across the room lifts his head from his backpack and looks up. Hoookay, he's no Hot Brother, but he definitely does not cause me any eye strain if you know what I mean.

Yes. Human interaction. Human interaction can stay.

4

I GET THIS PUMPKIN RAVIOLI BECAUSE BIANCA'S JUST GETTING A salad, and I know it's important that I eat more than she does. I've done that *who can eat less?* game with reluctant (or unaware) participant Disco Dykes, and I don't want her feeling like she has to compete with me. For all their (now obviously apparent) faults, the Dykes were really good with the eating disorder thing, always telling me I looked beautiful and trying to be these role models of eating and accepting their bodies, when of course they were all better-looking than me (Rachel especially, tall, Japanese, perfect—it figures we live in the white capital of Whiteland and my best friend is not only ten times more beautiful than me but also nonwhite to boot) so it wasn't really hard for them, but whatever. I'm really trying not to hate people for being pretty.

Especially because right now I can just fall back on a kindergartner's strategy of hating people because they're more talented, because goddamn. Bianca and James have been doing theater since they were tiny, and even though I didn't hear him sing, I can tell by his speaking voice that he's got to be decent, and being related to syrup-voiced Bianca has got to be a good sign. No idea if Mason's at that level, but he spits out credentials like he generally doesn't think they're a big deal, and hi, I'm Etta and I go to dance class.

"So how'd you guys meet?" I say.

Bianca says, "I was born, and James was like, there."

I say, "Oh, shut up, you."

She grins, and it makes the restaurant seem even warmer. I like it here. It's a little outside of town in the direction (away from Fremont, and Omaha, and general civilization) that I don't typically go, but maybe I need to start venturing further into the cornfield wastelands. Topically, the walls are painted with kind of creepily realistic pictures of farmers, like we're supposed to believe they're harvesting our food as we sit here. But this ravioli is really, really good, and after two months in recovery I'm just now getting to the point where I can genuinely enjoy food (while frantically calculating calories in my head, yeah. I'm not a superhero. Unless ridiculously precise food-math counts as a superpower).

"I met James at day camp when we were goddamn infants," Mason says. He curses, the siblings don't. I've figured out from the way they bowed their heads before they ate, all subtle, in unison, that they're definitely religious, and I've figured out from the way that James holds his fork—because come on it's not like I don't know my shit in this department—that he is definitely gay.

I say, "That's like me and my best friend. We were like betrothed at birth or something."

"Does she do theater too?" Mason says.

I shake my head. "We did kiddie dance classes together, but she was never really into it. Meanwhile I latched on to it and never stopped."

"Oh, so you're a dancer."

Shut it down! "I'm so completely not a dancer. I just do dance classes. You have to be good to be a dancer." I don't know why I'm saying this, really, because the truth is . . . I'm pretty damn good. It's the same way I used to pretend I ate a lot, I think. What if someday they see me dance and they think I'm not good? I have to start letting them down now. Jesus, I'm psychotic.

Bianca says, "I can't dance at all."

"I'm seriously hoping it's not a big part of the audition," Mason says, which maybe pisses me off a little because hello we just said that was what I was good at? Okay, maybe we kind of didn't. Maybe I avoided praise like a pussy. Shut up.

I look around the room just to have something else to do and my eyes fall on this waitress a few tables down. She's tallish, blond, hair in a bun but falling out and tucked behind her ears. Her uniform's a little wrinkled and she looks flustered, tired, but she's still sweet with her table, I can tell, refilling their water glasses and talking to them, smiling.

"See something you like?" James says, which amuses me because he totally has no reason to think that I'm into chicks (we don't have a special way of holding our forks).

But whatever, screw it. "She looks like my ex-girlfriend," I say. "I thought it was her for a second. Which is stupid because she's in New York."

"Girlfriend, huh?" Mason says. He looks kinda deflated. Aw, kid.

"I go both ways," I say. "You know that whole thing about there being that misconception about bisexuals being sluts? Like, everyone thinks that just because we're into both we're into *everybody*?"

James says, "I do know that misconception." Of course ya do, gay boy.

"Yeah well I'm actually kind of a slut. I'm awesome for the community, obviously."

"Communities are overrated," he says. "Go for small groups at co-ops."

"Cheers to that." I stuff another bite of ravioli into my mouth. Bianca takes a tentative forkful of salad, and James gives her this encouraging little smile. He hasn't been pushing her, but he has been looking at her some through the meal, subtle but not secret, not like he thinks she isn't going to notice. They're kind of a beautiful thing, I think.

"So 'kind of a slut' equals a lot of ex-girlfriends, I'm guessing," Mason says.

"Mostly a lot of ex-non-girlfriends, but yeah, Danielle was a thing. I'm still so completely in love with her, it's immensely depressing. We plow on, whatever."

"Why'd you break up?"

"She moved. New York. Luckiest girl in the world. Her mom got some job. It was one of those very sad very special episodes of a sitcom." Not the musical kind.

"So you just broke up?"

"We tried, I visited a lot, but it's hard. I was always so damn tired because I wasn't eating and she was working two jobs plus school and busy all the time, so we wouldn't spend all that much time together, and we'd both get snippy and passive-aggressive about it and it was just kind of a shitshow. Anyway, madly in love six months later, it's okay. I live around it. My best friend Rachel gave me some Smiths CDs. Fills the void."

"We've never been to New York," James says.

"Shit, really? You're theater kids! It's the capital of the world!"

"And it's so expensive."

"Right, yeah . . ." I try to be sensitive about this shit, seriously, I try so hard, but I mess it up all the time. The truth is that I go to this rich private school, so I'm just used to people having money to throw around. I'm used to people living in houses that are way too big for them and I guess taking impromptu trips to New York. The fact that this Brentwood thing is a scholarship is obviously awesome because hey, saving money for other stuff, always awesome, but the hard part for me would definitely be getting into Brentwood, not paying for it. It's not that I'm not grateful for having all this damn money. Whenever I think about it, I obviously so am. It's just that I don't think about it very often. I need to put Post-its around reminding me or something.

And the Brentwood thing is okay right now. I'm sitting here listening to them trade stories of their botched auditions (and they've all gotten through to auditions, Bianca even to second round), and they want this so much more than I do. I'm going to have a good time prepping for auditions with them, I think, but really I'm here as a cheerleader.

Which is completely fine, because have I mentioned how I don't really have friends right now? I will cheer to the death! But for now I tip my head back and remember Danielle and me on some rooftop looking over the Hudson, and feeling very small and so big and loving, both at the same time.

"So there are two rounds of auditions?" I ask.

"Three, actually," Mason says. "One where it's a whole bunch of people and they have everyone sing just a few bars. I don't even know how the hell they figure out if they're any good just from that. And judging by some of the people who get through to second round, maybe they kind of can't."

"Second round is more you," James says. "Kind of a long time in there. They get a sense of your personality, and you bring your own music, obviously. And then third round you go to New York to meet with the freaking board of the school! That's our goal this time around."

"That's my goal, like, period," I say. "I mean, not Brentwood. Necessarily. Just New York."

"She's scared," James says. "If Brentwood were in Nebraska, she'd be going at it so much harder." He talks for Bianca a lot. At first it seemed a little controlling, I'll be honest, but as it keeps happening I'm getting the feeling it's more like they're psychics and he's just being her voice. The sad thing is that I can tell that he's pretty shy too; he's just better at pushing through it than she is. She's clammed up a little more than before, even, and she's kind of shoving her lettuce around on her plate and drifting off, looking at this lady farmer on the wall beside her who has big thighs and looks strong.

"I want to be this person who gets out," I say.

Mason says, "A-fucking-men. Sorry, Bee."

She smiles at him. "It's fine."

James says, "You didn't apologize to me!"

"You don't get sad about God like Bianca does." Mason turns back to me. "Anyway. Getting out of Nebraska."

I say, "Getting out of Nebraska is like the first dream a Nebraskan baby has."

He taps his glass against mine.

I say, "I've just attached all this cosmic significance to getting to New York, and whenever I'm here, I feel like that's so cliché and stupid, but when I'm there, it just feels like the only option, you know? I've just promised it to myself."

"You'll get there."

"I'll get there. Stuff is just becoming . . . I don't know. Intolerabler." I shake it off. "I need something to keep me going before I can get out. Really I just want to be in a motorcycle gang. I think everything wrong with me is repressed and misguided agitation about not being in a motorcycle gang." I think I'm kidding.

Bu then Mason says, "I have a motorcycle," and yeah, maybe I wasn't kidding that much, or maybe it's just that he's really damn cute and has been smiling at me all through dinner and that I have this feeling that I can get on this bike and go anywhere and that he will want to go too.

"Shut up."

"Seriously. I'll bring it to prep tomorrow and take you out after. How about that?"

How about that indeed.

"You got it."

5

EVERY OTHER WEDNESDAY WE HAVE THESE THINGS CALLED extension days, which should really be called reduction days, to be honest, because all you do is this long grueling version of one class the entire day. This week is calculus, and I'm a math kid, but seriously, no math kid needs seven hours of calculus and no girl in exile needs seven hours of just the same fifteen people, I'm pretty sure, no one in the whole world needs seven hours with the same fifteen people when one of them is Natasha.

She makes this big show of ignoring me but otherwise doesn't do anything because I guess picking on someone all by yourself is boring, and she's the only Dyke in this class. To all the other girls she's just, well, a Dyke, so for a little while it feels like we're kind of the same. We're both friendless and surrounded by nothing but math, but then on her way to the bathroom she snaps my bra so hard my skin's still burning when she gets back, so yeah, I'm guessing she didn't feel like joining me down here at the bottom of my totem pole. Whatever, I out-math her like it's my job.

The people in my chorus at the rec center aren't mean, exactly. They're not even *unfriendly*. It's just that they all go to school together. They're picking up conversations that started during fifth period or whatever and passing each other notes and whispering about *oh my god Lisa what a slut!* I slept with a girl named Lisa once. Today I wish I were friends with these guys just so I could find out of it's the same one.

We're singing Mendel right now, "Hallelujah Chorus," which is okay as far as choral music goes. It's got these gorgeous high notes, but I'm a mezzo, so those aren't mine. I sing these notes right in the middle, and the other mezzos find them no problem, while I have to hope my director remembers to play all the parts separately this time instead of jumping into playing all the harmonies and assuming we'll be able to pick our parts out ourselves. (God, where did these girls learn to pick these out themselves? Like, I can read music, I took piano when I was a kid, where are my superpowers?)

I reach for one of our highest notes and my voice breaks. Carolina next to me screws up her own note by laughing, ha *ha*.

I buckle down and get through Mendel, because after this I'm singing whatever I damn well please.

• • •

It would be nice if I had any idea what that was.

Mason says, "Maybe it'll help you, not having something specific in mind. Means you can go in there all open to anything at that first audition and not be thinking, *but I could sing my song so much better.*"

"What kind of stuff do they usually pick?" We're back in the practice room, and this time there's someone older than us coaching some people by the blackboard, and some people are listening and some people are off on their own, and then there's me and Mason stretched out on the floor because why not. James is looking through a songbook, Bianca flitting by his shoulder and flipping back and forth between different pages, pointing stuff out, making him nod.

Mason says, "Something hard, usually."

"Oh, good!"

He laughs. "It's all about attitude at this stage. Show you deserve to be there, and they'll believe you. The people auditioning you at this point are some low-level volunteers. You'll be fine."

"Are you nervous?"

He shrugs. Well, all right, thank you for keeping the conversation going, Mason. He's damn lucky he's cute.

Bianca laughs, louder than she talks, and slips a little on the floor. I can't believe I thought that girl was a dancer.

Mason smiles a little and stretches. He's slim, not skinny,

white and broad-shouldered and big-eyed. He's the kind of guy who I bet would look great onstage, and maybe that's the kind of thing he thinks about. "She's such a dork."

"Did you ever . . ."

He says "What?" like he genuinely has no clue how that sentence ends, come on, kid.

"You and Bianca."

"Me and *Bianca*? Like . . . as a thing? No no no no, God, I need to, like borax my brain now."

"Come on, she's cute."

"She's fourteen, and I've known her since she was three. She's like my little sister."

"How long has she been . . ."

"Yeah. I don't know. I didn't notice until last year. James says it's been going on longer than that. It wasn't exactly something he talked about. She was always skinny and she's been weird about food since she was little, always saying stuff gave her stomachaches and she wasn't hungry and asking for diet soda in her kiddie cup at restaurants. I don't know. I don't get how all this works, I guess."

"The eating disorder thing?"

"Yeah, just . . . you know. Why?"

"We go through tons and tons of therapy trying to figure out 'why.' Everyone wants it to be this same exact reason for everybody, like, *oh, shit, if only I hadn't eaten that house paint in 2002 I'd be eating like a normal person!*"

"You stupid kid."

"Right?"

He smiles. At me.

"So how's she doing?" I ask.

"I don't know. I guess since she's doing group and stuff, we're all supposed to talk about how well she's doing, but she's still not eating, so I guess I'm kind of failing to see what the big deal about group is."

"Yeah, they don't force-feed you unless you do inpatient."

"But you . . . I mean, you eat."

I'm going to choose to believe that he's getting that from the fact that I ate last night and not because I'm clearly not wasting away, because that's what a healthy and sane individual would believe. "Yeah. I've been in treatment longer than she has, though. I mean, in our group at least."

"Was it hard?"

"Of course."

"Maybe you could mentor her."

"I think maybe we . . . I don't know. We're coming at this from different places, judging by stuff we've said in group. God, I should not be telling you this shit."

"You're telling me about you. It's okay."

And then he puts his hand on my back. The small of my back, just kind of . . . puts his hand there. It's big and warm.

I say, "I don't think she'd have that voice still if she'd been throwing up for a few years."

"Oh."

"I know. It's gross. Shit."

He taps his fingers over my spine.

My spine. He doesn't know he's doing it.

I lean back into his hand. "Motorcycle tonight, right?"

He nods and sits up, gives one of my dreads a little tug. "Motorcycle tonight."

The four of us (oh God, I'm a "four of us") are leaving the community center by way of the damn third floor, and ugh, shit, I forgot I lingered after last time and that's probably why I didn't see Miss Michelle's class letting out, but here they are now, tights and leg warmers and gym bags, pretty, teeny little white girls (this is why I thought Bianca might be a dancer) spilling out into the hallways, and more than a few of them give me a "Hi, Etta," or at least nod in a way that isn't all hateful, so all in all, these past five minutes have had more positive interactions with more humans than I've had in, like, months, but I'm still trying to get Bianca and Mason and James out of here as quickly as possible—*Okay, keep moving, nothing to see*—because really the last thing I want to do is talk about this.

And then of course, of *course*, Miss Michelle goes, "Etta?" And damn it, why can't I have some name she wouldn't immediately know was me from hearing the girls, you know? No one's going to be like, *Etta who?*

"Uh, hi, Miss Michelle."

"How are you, sweetheart? God, it's been almost a year, hasn't it?"

"Yeah, that sounds right. Uh, how have you been?"

"Oh, same old, same old. One of my girls broke her ankle, so I'm sending a whole bunch of them over with flowers and they're being catty about it."

"Catty dancers? I never."

"How's BN?"

Uggggh. "It's great. It's really great."

"I miss you like hell here, but you know what? Seeing you in *Cinderella* in August made me so glad we let you go!"

"Oh. . . . You came to *Cinderella*?"

"Of course! I didn't see you in *The Nutcracker*, though!"

"Right, I had to drop out, kind of last minute. It was a medical thing." This is so valid that it shouldn't even be a lie, except that it is.

"Oh, I'm sorry to hear that. Are you doing better now?"

"Yeah, I am." All right. Not lying still feels good. Maybe I'm not going to hell or whatever.

"Will I see you in *Alice*? When's that, April?"

"Oh, maybe. I haven't auditioned yet." Half lie! That'd be that "yet." There will be no *Alice* audition in my future.

"I'm sure you'll get in. You're still the most talented girl I've taught, Etta."

Oh God this is the most awkward thing I've ever experienced. This is Crowning Moment of Awkward. "Thank you,

Miss Michelle. I really appreciate it. I need to get going. . . ."

"Right, of course. *Merde!*"

"Ha, yeah. *Merde.*"

I usher Bianca, James, and Mason down the hallway and down the stairs.

"Did you just say 'shit' in French?" Mason says.

"Yeah, it's . . ." *A ballet thing.* "Not important. Let's get out of here."

We pile into James's pickup truck with Mason's motorcycle in the bed. I sit in the backseat next to Bianca and swallow, and swallow, and swallow.

"You okay?" she whispers.

I nod and close my eyes and tell myself what I'm hearing in my head is Mendel, or Sondheim.

Is anything but the damn "Dance of the Sugar Plum Fairy."

6

"HELMET," MASON SAYS, SNAPPING HIS INTO PLACE.

"Please, I know. This isn't a Lifetime movie."

We're on a silent road by a cornfield, like that's at all descriptive when you're in damn Nebraska. The town has started to grow in the past thirty years, hence the snobby girls' school, as a lot of rich people are moving here for some reason I still haven't figured out—my mom runs social work which is probably why she's weirdly supportive of my goals to be a destitute Bohemian—but the town is still like 95 percent corn-fields. This time of year, it's just a corn graveyard, dried-up creepy stalks and dry dirt. No snow yet.

Bianca and James are waiting by his pickup truck. Well, James is, leaning against the hood, looking up at the stars like he's counting them. Bianca's inside the car shivering and looking at the dashboard.

"All right, climb on!"

I haul myself onto the seat and press myself into him. I'm suddenly all conscious of my body, how my boobs and stomach must feel against his back.

So I'm a person with aspirations of being in a motorcycle gang who has never actually been on a motorcycle before. He takes off, and I wasn't prepared for how much I would feel it through my whole body, vibrate with it, somehow feel like I'm causing it to happen.

It's pretty amazing. Way to go with those based-on-nothing dreams, Etta. Good taste.

I squeeze him around the waist a little tighter than I need to as we speed up and the dead corn blurs into gray-brown wallpaper. The headlights make the road look blue, and the helmet hushes everything, and as much as I'm enjoying being wrapped around him, a part of me wishes I were alone, that it were just me and this thing that I have no idea how to drive, yeah, but besides that just the road and me and however many stars there are.

But being here with him, this cute boy I just met yesterday, this cute boy who knows I'm not good at food or ex-girlfriends and still wants me pressed against his back . . . I am just not really complaining, is the thing.

Especially when he pulls over the motorcycle and tugs me into some dead corn and kisses me, hands big around my ears and neck and pulling me close.

Not complaining, not at all.

I like him.

"So. Um." Bianca's out of the car now, wearing James's coat and Mason's and my scarves. The boys are drinking beers by the trunk. Like one each, this really is not going to be a Lifetime movie. But what up, good little Christian boy! Iiiinteresting.

I tuck her under my arm a little and rub her head to warm her up. She leans into me. "Yeah?" I say.

"Is Mason maybe gonna be your boyfriend?"

"Ha! I don't know. Aw, I'm not laughing at you. I just don't think that much about boys."

"Or girls?" She's totally interested. Sweet girl.

"Or girls. Not with dating, anyway." *Anymore*, my brain goes all melodramatically, but really it's not like I lost my faith in love after Danielle or something. To quote *Rent*, "It's not that kind of movie, honey."

The boys come back around to stand with us and start talking about something singing-related with words I don't even know, so I drift away a few paces and twist my feet up on the ground. I get up on my toes and look down at my ankles. I haven't been en pointe in months. I don't know if I can go back to it, that I have the ankle strength anymore. Not that I would. I don't do that anymore.

But it feels good, having this extra half inch, holding myself up. I go to the cornfield and dig my toe in and turn a few pirouettes. It's hard to do in the dirt, but I kind of like the give. Makes me feel strong. I focus on the side mirror of the truck to keep from getting dizzy. I like how my dreadlocks feel when I whip my head around; I always used to get in trouble for those unless they were pulled up in this tight little bun, and sometimes even then. Black girls aren't supposed to be ballerinas, and I guess if they are, they're supposed to have their hair relaxed. (My mom's always suggesting I do that, since she does and Kristina does, and she's like *wouldn't you like to look less "urban"*? Like she would know urban if it bit her in the ass, and I'm like *wouldn't you like to fuck off?* and it turns out we would not, thank you!) But conveniently I'm not a ballerina, so I'll just enjoy my dreads hitting me in the face for these impromptu pirouettes.

I turn three before I realize they're watching me. Mason laughs and says, "What are you doing?"

"Pirouettes," I say, and what the hell, I turn a few more. It's painful in my bare feet, but I haven't tried one in at least two months and I sort of can't believe I can still do them. I feel warm and terrified all at once.

"So that's what that was, right?" James says. "You do ballet."

"Hey, I told you I danced."

Bianca is little-kid excited. "You said '*danced*.' You didn't say you were a ballerina!"

"I am so incredibly not a ballerina." I sit down in the dirt. "I was *once* a ballerina. Sort of. I was once a person who did ballet. Now I do occasional pirouettes in cornfields, apparently."

Bianca says, "I watch those girls practice all the time. They're *so* good."

"What, the ones in the community center?"

"Yeah."

"The ones we just saw get out?"

"Yeah!"

"No no no. I mean . . ." Great, there's nowhere I can go without sounding catty. "I mean, they're *fine*. I was their level when I was like . . . I don't know. A few years ago."

"So . . . that wasn't your class?"

"No, it was, and then I did private with Miss Michelle, and then she told me to audition at BN."

Mason says, "What's BN?"

"Ballet Nebraska. In Omaha."

"Is that like a big deal?" he says. "That sounds like a big deal."

I shrug and sift dirt through my hands. "I quit in October."

"Why'd you stop?" James says.

"Look at me."

He's quiet for a second. Then he says, "You're beautiful."

Bianca nods.

God, I missed friends.

"My choreographer at BN told me I needed to lose some weight, and, like, no shit. Look, I'm really not hating on how I look. I'm just saying that objectively and honestly I do not look like a ballerina. Being five feet tall doesn't help much, and not being skinny doesn't help much either. So my . . . I decided it would be a good idea for me to quit. For my mental health and stuff."

"That must be so hard," Bianca says quietly. "Not being able to do it."

"We plow on."

"Yeah," she says. "We plow on."

Bianca is singing later, just gently to herself, still sounding like it's the easiest thing in the damn world, twirling around on Mason's back. James is watching all fondly, and I think about how much I've always loved seeing Kristina and Rachel get along on the brief occasions when they do, and how awesome it would have been long-term to see my two favorite people just enjoying each other's company. What's holding Bianca and Mason together, presumably, is how much they love James, and what an amazing mind-trip that must be, to be loved so intensely that it brings other people together.

I go and stand with him and he hands me a beer. "I'm kind of surprised you drink," I say.

"Just with Mason. And he doesn't drink all that much either. But you know, warmish night, what the hell, right?"

"Ooh, look who curses."

"Just not in front of her."

"I love how close you guys are."

"Yeah, she's my universe. Stuff was never great with our parents. We kind of glued together." He takes a pack of cigarettes out of his pocket. "Want one?"

"No thanks."

"Mind if I do?"

"Go for it."

"Awesome, thanks. She hates it."

"She's, uh. A good girl."

He laughs. "That she is. I mean, I try. Jesus and all that."

"Mmm-hmm."

"I don't think it's that I don't believe it as much as she does, because I think I actually do. It just means more to her, you know? It's been really good for her these past few months, something to cling to. She needs something."

"How'd she get into recovery?"

"I'd been begging for a hundred damn years, but finally Mom kind of broke down and cried, and that pushed it. My dad's still acting like it doesn't exist."

"My dad likes to act like I don't exist."

"Ooh, they should get together. Racquetball."

"You really are gay."

He groans. "Gaaawd. You can tell?"

"I'm kind of an expert in my field. Mason's the first straight guy I've talked to in, like, six months, excluding the one I slept with."

"I don't really hide it, y'know? But I haven't . . . told anyone."

"Whoa, not even Bianca?"

"No. I don't think she has any idea."

"Wow."

"She's . . . I mean, obviously stuff's rough for her right now, and I don't want to . . . shatter her. This gay stuff, it's complicated for her. She obviously thinks everyone has the right to be happy, and she obviously knows that everyone's picking and choosing parts of the Bible all the damn time. But . . ."

"I don't really know any religious people."

"We're not all assholes."

"No, I didn't think you were." Except maybe I kind of did. I've been raised in this science-above-all-else family, so even though I *know* that religious people aren't all holding signs outside abortion clinics or whatever, sometimes it's easy to forget. Maybe I watch too much TV.

I say, "So you're, what, never going to tell her?"

"Well, she doesn't eat, maybe she'll die soon."

"You're a horrible person."

"You can only lie awake crying about it for so many nights before you *have* to make jokes about it, you know?"

"Yeah, my best friends and I had so many starving jokes

near the end of it. Sometimes you just have to pretend your life is a dark comedy."

He takes a pull on his cigarette. "Sometimes life *is* a freaking dark comedy. Near the end of what?"

"Oh. I don't know. Un-recovery. Our friendships. Whatever."

"Not friends anymore?"

I shrug. "It's complicated."

He doesn't push. "I think people overthink things," he says. "I think *stopping being friends* is a really weird concept. Why is it something you'd give that much thought to? I don't even understand breaking up with boyfriends. How do you wake up in the morning and just analyze something to the point where you decide it's over?"

"Well, sometimes people treat you like shit, I guess."

"Like your friends did." Apparently he is pushing.

"Complicated. In their opinion I hurt them first. Vomited on their belief or whatever."

"I thought you were against vomiting!"

I finish my beer. "Yeah, well, maybe that's why we're not friends anymore."

"You miss them?" he asks.

"I miss being part of something."

"Well." He looks out at Bianca and Mason. Mason is putting her down. She's blowing on her hands and complaining that she wants coffee. "Maybe now you are," he says.

7

THE BOYS AREN'T INTERESTED IN COFFEE, SO THEY DROP ME AND
Bianca off with my car and we go together. She was thinking Starbucks or something, but come on, sweetie, hasn't she
heard of the only cool place in all of Schuyler? It's this retro
little coffeehouse, so of course the Dykes loved it even though
it isn't technically seventies, just some hodgepodge of decades
with fifties music and neon chairs. It's always loud and full of
the fifteen people in the town who have piercings. Bianca, for
all her quiet good-girlness, curls up in a chair like a cat and
cups her coffee to her chest and looks comfortable.

"Did you have fun?" she asks, which is so cute, like it was
a little night planned for my benefit. I hope it wasn't. I hope
we can do that a lot.

"I really completely did."

"Yay!" God, she's a baby.

"How's the coffee, you warming up?"

"Mmm-hmm. It's good. Starbucks always burns mine."

"What the hell, Starbucks, what good are you. Uh . . . that's okay, right?"

"Insulting Starbucks? It's kind of like insulting my third parent, but I think I'll recover."

"Ha. 'Hell.'"

"Oh, yeah, of course. I don't mind what you say. I just try not to."

"You don't think I'm going to hell?"

"I make it a rule not to decide who's going to hell. I think if I were God I'd have a cool beard or something."

"You're cute."

She smiles.

"Not sure how cute you'd be with a beard, though."

She closes her eyes and hums a few measures of "Unchained Melody" with the jukebox. (Not even fifties, why does this place even try, so adorable.) Then Bianca opens her eyes and says, "I love that there are so many snow globes here! I love snow globes. And I love this song."

"Me too. My mom sings it while she bakes."

"I wish my mom baked. Etta. Etta. What are you singing for your audition?"

"Uh, shit, I don't know. You're doing 'Let's Hear It for the Boy'?"

"Uh-huh. I've done it every audition since I was, like, sentient. I don't even like *Footloose*."

"Yeah, who does."

"Right? Just that song."

"That's how I feel about— Okay, I don't want your look of horror, so brace yourself."

She grips the armrests.

"That's how I feel about *Wicked*."

"What? No. No!"

"It's so overrated. I'm sorry. It's not *bad*, it's just so incredibly overhyped."

"Noooo."

"I'm forgiving for musicals too, I swear! I like *Avenue Q* even though it's stupid as hell. I like *Rent* even though it's a white construction."

"What's your favorite?"

"*Billy Elliot*, maybe."

She groans.

"Yeah, I know, not much in it for a singer. Plus . . . Wait, have you seen it?"

"No, just heard the sound track."

"Oh, yeah, the sound track is so shitty. You have to see it in person. It's all about the dancing."

She shrugs. "I don't really *get* dancing, I guess. I mean, I want to . . ."

"Ever seen a ballet?"

She shakes her head.

"Ohhh God, okay, we need to table this discussion. I will accept your dismissal of *Billy Elliot* after you've seen a better dancing show. Right now it's winning its category just by, like, default."

"I like *My Fair Lady*."

"Boooring. Just choose *Sound of Music*, why don't you."

She laughs with her head tipped back. It's pretty and so much older than she is. Rachel laughs like that.

"Did you always love ballet?" she says.

"Yeah, ever since I was tiny. I was this little overachiever in my class, it was ridiculous. But I ended up changing ballet schools all the time, following different teachers."

"Stage mom?"

"Oh, hell no, just an indulgent one, I guess. By the time I was like eight she was letting me tell her what the best programs were and just following my lead. You?"

"I don't know," she says. "I guess. My parents never performed or anything, but my mom has this really nice voice, so I guess they pour it all into us."

"Gotta love that non-pressure."

"Right? So . . . you quit because they told you to lose weight? They shouldn't have done that."

"It's not like it was this constant spoken thing, you know, everyone telling me to lose weight or whatever. It wasn't like that. My teacher said something this one time and I went crying to Rachel about it and . . . I don't know, we talked about it, and she was right, it wasn't just this one teacher saying something. It was the whole system of ballet, the . . . I mean, the *discipline* of it. I didn't fit. Depressingly literally."

"So . . . you quit because Rachel told you to."

"It's that obvious, huh?"

She smiles. "Maybe a little."

I don't know how I'm thinking about this girl. Bianca. I'm not sure why I can't stop watching her and I'm not sure any of the possibilities are okay, because there's no answer that makes her not a severely eating-disordered straight *fourteen-year-old*, so I smile at her a little and then look away and sip my coffee.

She says, "So, um," and she doesn't even need to say anything else before I know she's doing some mind reading of my creepy half-lesbian brain, and shit, shit, she knows I was looking. "You, uh, are attracted to girls?"

Damn. I really wasn't looking at her like that, I swear. "Yeah. And boys too."

"So I guess it's hard from both sides."

She's the only person who's ever figured that out on her own. I put my cup down.

"Yeah," I say. "Yeah. I'm never gay enough and never straight enough."

"Sounds scary."

"Just lonely, really."

"So do you, like . . . How did you *know*?"

"It was finding out that everyone else *wasn't* bisexual that was the shock, honestly. I thought it was like . . . you know, how some guys like blondes better. I thought that some people like girls better but that everyone likes both to *some* degree, you know? And I guess I thought people just usually married the other one because it was easier. And you know what?"

"What."

"I kind of thought that maybe a bunch of them were cowards who just didn't want to tell their parents. I guess I knew it was something my parents would disapprove of before I knew it was a *thing*."

"It's been hard? With your parents?"

The truth is I feel shitty about complaining because I know so many people have it much worse. My mom hasn't kicked me out. She hasn't told me she disapproves. No, she told me she loved me and accepted me and of course it's okay with her, nothing would ever make her less proud of me. Yeah, well, talk is cheap, and apparently . . . Apparently when you're sitting on the couch trying to talk about your new girlfriend and you just get these averted eyes and cleared throats and changed topics, when you invite the girl over for dinner like she *told* you you were allowed to and she spends the entire time talking around both of you and giving you the occasional awkward smile while she directs every single comment to your sister instead . . . well, apparently silence is cheap too.

"Yeah," I say. "It's been rough."

She stirs her coffee idly with her pinky finger. She says, "I don't think my parents would be okay with it."

"They're religious, yeah?"

"Uh-huh. Not as much as me in actual . . . thought, I don't think, but they're so ingrained in that church culture and everything. I don't even like church all that much. I like the singing and the stained-glass, but mostly . . . mostly I just like, you know, me and God, at the end of the day. None of the middlemen or whatever. But I don't . . . I mean, you understand. I don't think you're bad or anything."

"I like you," I say.

"I like you, too."

"My mom isn't religious. She votes Democrat. She loves gay people until there's one sitting at her dinner table." I wave my hand a little. "I'm not gay."

"If James ever told my parents . . ."

"Oh, whoa, okay. You . . . I mean, you think James is . . ."

"Come on," she says. "Obviously James is."

"And that's . . . I mean, you're okay with it?"

The pause is too long.

I say, "I'm not . . . It is different. When it's sitting at your dinner table. I'm not judging. It's allowed to be hard for you."

"It'd be easier if he'd just *tell* me," Bianca says. "If he'd trust me with it."

"How sure are you that he's gay?" I'm just testing the waters, I think. It is not my place to give him away.

"Twenty thousand percent. Or, like, . . . sixty. I don't know." She plays with her hair, and I see some fall out in her hand. Baby.

"He loves you," I say.

"I know. Of course."

"He's just trying to protect you."

"Maybe if he didn't . . . didn't act like it was something I'm supposed to be protected from . . ."

"You're a smart girl, y'know that?"

"Yeah. Perfectionist, hypercritical, anorexic. I'm so not interesting."

I try to do this sympathetic little nod, but the truth is that my brain is *stuck* on the word "anorexic" because Jesus Christ, the size of this girl, she's got to fit all those stupid little criteria. This girl is actually *anorexic*, and we're sitting here discussing musicals and gay boys like we're normal people, when all I want to be doing—God, all I *should want to be doing*—is grabbing her by the skinny damn wrists and begging her to tell me all her secrets. Why is it that no matter what way I look at this eating disorder thing, I'm always doing it wrong?

"Maybe he needs some gay friends," Bianca says, in this measured, neutral little voice that makes me smile. "I have Bible friends."

"Everyone needs some gay friends, but it's not . . . I don't know. I guess I'm questioning that habit of segregating. And come on, you do musical theater. You can't tell me you don't know gay people."

"No, of course we do. We just . . . I mean, we don't, I mean *James* doesn't have a group of just people like that."

"Like I did."

"Uh-huh."

"I . . . I don't know. I really only ever liked one person in my little group." It's not that simple, though. Like, no shit, Rachel and I were the closest, but it's not like I didn't ever do phone calls with Titania or go over to Isabel's house just us. Natasha and I were into old sitcoms in a way the others totally weren't, so we'd bond over that, and when Isabel's parrot died, I was the one who was all over that shit, and while the others were going, *I don't get it it's just a bird,* I was designing floral arrangements. I was good at being a friend. I was just really good at it. But the thing is that they were *too.* If there had been some prior hint of it, some time now where I could look back and be like, *Well they'd always been dropping clues they'd someday turn on me and treat me like shit,* maybe this would be easier. But that's not what happened. We fought like normal friends, and there was always a little tension between me and Natasha just because we were these girls who probably wouldn't have been friends without the gay thing who were pushed together and learned to love each other maybe without learning to like each other, whatever, but we were close. We were best friends for all of high school.

And now all of a sudden I'm dropped, and I don't care how much bullshit you hear all the time about *some girls are just bitches*, because, you know, no, they are not *just bitches*, they were my best friends for three years and this doesn't make *sense*, and yeah, a part of me still thinks Rachel is going to pick up the phone.

"I don't miss them because I miss gay friends, you know?" I say. "I don't even miss them because I miss *friends*. I miss them because I miss . . ."

"Them."

She's good at filling in sentences. People sit around talking for her when really she could be filling in all our sentences.

"Yeah," I say. "I miss them. Or I miss her."

And then I take a sip of my coffee and the bell on the door chimes and the song switches and I look up and who just walked in, who the hell could have *just walked in*, but Rachel.

Rachel.

Beach vacations with our moms, swimmer's ear, snow cones.

Broken hearts, chipped nail polish.

Making out against mango stands when there were straight people around.

Practicing sex positions.

Always coming back to her.

She was never my girlfriend. She was never my sister. I

say she was my best friend because there is no word for *every.* *damn. thing.*

There's no word for a girl you've seen almost every day for fourteen years who still makes your heart race every time she walks into a room.

I don't even know if I say anything to Bianca. I just know that I'm standing here at the counter while Rachel waits for her drink. I always feel like such a little kid next to her. She has eight inches on me and hair that hangs flat and perfect down to my eyes. I could hide behind her like it was nothing. But she never let me. *You're a star, Ett,* she'd say. *And this is not an eclipse.* I didn't tell her eclipses don't have anything to do with stars. I never listened very hard to the words when she talked, not really. When you're friends with someone that long, you don't have to.

"Rachel?"

It's such a *word.* It's so *sharp.* It never really felt like a name that fit her, and that always made me love it so much more.

I didn't know if she was pretending to ignore me, but when her head snaps up and she looks at me, I know immediately that she really didn't know I was there.

I know a few other things too.

I know that I've been bouncing around waiting for her for months. I know we haven't had a single conversation since that night I met Ben at Cupcake, just a few *Rachels?* from me cut off by a load of *just leave her alone, Etta, okay?*s from the Dykes. I know that I've just been on pins and damn needles ready to find out if she's the leader of all of this, if she's the head bitch in charge of ruining my life, or if she's—please, please—letting them run the show right now, letting them make all the decisions to freeze me out. Maybe she was even a little mad at me at first but she isn't anymore. Rachel's either going to be the angriest of the whole group or not angry at all, and how have I been sitting around with no idea how this person, this person I know every single damn inch of, is feeling about me?

Especially when now she's looking at me and the answer is so obvious.

I hurt her.

I fucking hurt her.

And the fact that I hurt her—look, I'm not forgetting this, not even ignoring it—is stupid, because I *didn't do anything wrong*. But oh my God this is Rachel and who cares if it was a mistake or it wasn't a mistake, because it shouldn't have had to have been a mistake because I didn't do anything *wrong*, and who cares if this betrayal is in her head or if it's legitimate and standing right the hell in front of her, here I am, here I am, and I hurt my best friend.

And I've been lying around feeling like the only damn victim here.

God, this sucks.

"Hey, Etta," she says.

I haven't heard her this quiet since she had laryngitis in ninth grade.

I have no idea what to say.

"Caramel apple latte?" I say.

She just looks at me.

"I didn't hear," I said. "I just, you know, guessed. They're only here for another couple of weeks." Rachel's diabetic, but she'll always take an extra shot for the caramel apple lattes.

"Right."

The punch line of this conversation is that we both got A's in public speaking.

"I heard you were sick," I say.

She shrugs her hair over her shoulder. "I'm not, really. I'm better practically. I just couldn't really deal with school right now."

"Because of me?"

She sighs, but it doesn't sound sarcastic. It really doesn't. "Why would it be you, Etta? Nothing's changed in months."

"Then why does it sound like it's me?"

"Because I'm working through it. I'm trying to get over it, okay?"

"You mean get over me."

"No, Ett, I don't."

If I could see over her shoulder, I'm sure I could see Bianca watching us. God, I wonder what she's thinking. I wonder if she thinks I'm completely losing at this conversation.

Jesus, I'm talking about winning a conversation? This isn't public speaking. This is my *best friend*.

Rachel shoves her hands into the pockets of her parka. "Do you have any idea what the past few months have been like for me?"

"You haven't exactly been cluing me in, no."

"My parents are asking me, *so are you going to date a boy now*, all hopeful and shit. The Dykes can't look at this as anything but some big political whateverthehell and God, they're . . . and I am still trying to deal with the fact that maybe me and my best friend and our wives aren't going to grow old together, okay? Don't laugh at me."

"I'm not." I'm not.

"I don't . . . You didn't do anything wrong," she says, and despite everything, I still want to pick these words up and frame them. "But this isn't . . . I didn't . . ." She shakes her head fast and shoves her hair behind her ears. "It's not what you did, and I don't blame you, it's just I had this picture in my head of who you were and what our lives were going to be like, and now maybe it's not going to be like that and maybe I'm being stupid but I just . . . I need *time*, okay? I know you think this is stupid, but I'm fucking *shattered*."

"Ben and I broke up, though. It wasn't even *anything*."

"But that's just one guy. How am I supposed to know this was just a onetime thing?"

And what am I supposed to say here? Because I'm not going to tell her I'm not going to date guys ever again. I'm not going to tell her this is some phase. He was the first guy I slept with. I liked it. I always knew I would. I'm not going to pretend the reason Ben and I weren't anything is because he was a guy. It was just because my particular relationship with that guy didn't particularly turn out to be anything.

I'm not going to lie to her. She's my best friend, and I was making out with a guy all of an hour and a half ago.

But if I did lie to her, if I just *could*, then maybe there wouldn't be any more ranch-dressing condoms in my locker, you know?

But no. No. "You always knew this," I say. "I always told all of you that I was bi, and you all just ignored it." (Natasha used to say shit she thought was so funny, *die-sexual, one foot in the grave*.)

Rachel says, "God, I must sound like a fucking . . ."

"Heterophobe? Yeah, you do, and it's not really cute and alternative when you're pointing it at me."

"Don't you miss us, though?"

"We should still be able to goddamn be friends."

"Not us. Not the Dykes. The . . . community. Look, you and I both know that you didn't just stop going to Pride because you didn't fit in anymore. How can you really be part of this if you're dating a guy?"

"Yeah, well, how can Pride really be Pride when they send

me passive-aggressive emails about *why don't you stop coming,* that's the freaking reason, Rachel."

"They shouldn't have done that," she says quietly.

"Yeah, well."

"Straight people have still given us more shit than Pride ever could."

I heard a bitch in my gym class today mumbling to some other bitch in my gym class that *good thing Etta's ugly, since she's apparently sleeping with guys now.* Rachel really doesn't need to remind me that there's not a single group that likes me.

She says, "But that's kind of what I'm talking about, y'know? The community is never going to think of straight people the same way—".

"Bisexual, Rachel, I'm bisexual, it's a fucking *word.*"

"But the whole world isn't going to see you like that. They're going to see you as gay or they're going to see you as straight, depending on who's holding your hand, so can you just . . ."

Can you hold my hand.

She doesn't have to say it.

She'll never be my girlfriend. It's not like that.

But we were supposed to grow old together.

She thought she knew me.

"At some point you're going to make a choice," Rachel says. "And whatever that choice is, you're going to lose one half of this bi thing, and you've already come out, okay, and you have the whole community on our side and we'll get you back in there and you have us, okay, you have me, we can take on anything, right? You and me. And you guys broke up, so good, that's done, so we can . . . we can rebuild from here, okay?"

"Ray . . ."

"I need some air." She's breathing hard. She does this sometimes.

Her drink comes up, and I hand it to her. It's hot chocolate. Oh.

"I need to go outside," she says. "Can you come?"

"I'm with a friend," I say. "Sit with us?".

She turns around. "Who is she?"

"Bianca. She's . . ." I don't feel right about saying Bianca's in my group, not without her permission. ". . . auditioning for something with me."

"Yeah? You're doing an audition?"

"Uh-huh."

"That's . . . that's great, Etta. Not ballet, right?"

Rachel was the one who helped me bury my toe shoes in the backyard. Rachel said ballet was a symbol of everything that's holding me back and tying me down and telling me that I have to look and be a certain way. She said ballet was making me miserable and I need to be triumphant and throw it away and that that means I will triumph over it instead of it triumphing over me. She said the tenets of ballet are discipline and poise and body control and *that's not you, Etta, you should never be restrained like this.*

Probably right, you know?

"No," I say. "No, not ballet."

"I don't want to interrupt. . . ."

"It's okay, just . . ."

She shakes her head and says, "I'm a mess," and yeah, she kind of is. She dabs her eyes on the cuff of her glove and says, "I'll see you, Etta."

"Can I call you?"

"I don't know."

"Right."

"I'll see you."

"Etta?"

"Not now, Kristina." I'm busy kicking my boots off into the corner and hating everything. I managed to act normal and bubbly through dropping Bianca off, but I'm tired and I'm not normal and bubbly and all I want to do is eat an entire box of Oreos and shove my hand down my throat so yeah, not at my damn best right now, I love you, little sis, but ten minutes, maybe? (Not to binge-purge, just to calm myself down. Promise.)

"Okay, but can I just ask you one thing, though?" She's standing there in the doorway of my room, all nervous. Kristina's taller and bigger than me, but there's something about her that's really small, something that I want to take and fold into my shirt and keep safe, and I need to remember that that still exists even when I'm wishing that everything else in the world didn't.

I sit down on my bed. "Heavily" is just so the right word right now. "Yeah."

"Am I ugly?"

"What? Come here."

She's on the bed in a second, all squished into my side. "I really thought this boy from Saint Anthony's liked me, and then no, he's dating *Claire Bowman* all of a sudden, and he was not dating her last week, and guess who he was IMing with four nights out of last week, uh, hint, not Claire Bowman."

"Messed up."

"Guys always like you." It's so weird, all the different things people in my life tell me about me.

"You should try pushing your boobs in their face. They like that."

"Huh. Yeah."

I rest my head on her shoulder. "I'm building on this theory that Saint Em's is actually a torture chamber that they built for young female delinquents and that you and I did something very horrible when we were children that we don't remember. And now we're being punished. Intensely."

She laughs a little. "You can't blame Em's for everything."

"I think probably I can. No, but seriously, you can't tell me that girls who aren't stuck in a tube for eight hours a day with *just* other girls, all of whom have the money for whatever the hell plastic surgery and designer whateverthehell it could take to make them look a hundred times better than any fifteen-year-old is supposed to, are having as rough a time with this shit as we are."

"I'm just bitching." She buries her face in my side. "I'm okay."

God, I wish I were just bitching. I wish I were okay. Talking to Rachel has brought this all to this gross peak in my head, and I'm turning all the little bits of shit I've faced lately—and let's not even pretend most of it isn't these pointed silent treatments punctuated by unpredictable verbal jabs from the Dykes—into this pattern, into this big overarching comment on my current existence.

I hate Nebraska because Nebraska is where I am.

But there's more important shit going on. I say, "You're freaking beautiful is what you are, okay?"

"How come I can't get a boyfriend?"

"Because boyfriends are stupid."

"Shitty answer."

"Yeah, I know. It'll happen."

"You smell like smoke."

"I should smell like smoke, bike exhaust, and coffee."

"Why is your life so much cooler than mine?"

"I forgot the stink of wasted talent and desperation. I had chorus and this audition prep today too."

"Even when you were my age you were doing cool stuff."

"Yeah, well, I was Mom's lost cause, she let me do whatever. You've got to be sweet."

"I am not a sweet person, is the problem."

I sit up and groan. "I have homework. If I'm so rebellious and cool, why do I have homework?"

"At least you don't have to spend a billion hours doing ballet practice anymore."

"Hey, you ever miss it?" I ask. We took lessons together when we were little. Kristina gave it up early, if "gave it up" means "lay on the floor in the hallway outside our class and shrieked and bailed and refused to go in." My baby girl is feisty.

"Miss what?" she says.

"Dancing."

She looks at me like I'm crazy.

"I know," I say. "Me neither."

"I mean, you have tap. So why would you."

"Exactly." Tap. Right.

You don't have to be skinny for tap.

(Apparently you don't have to love it either.)

8

CHICKEN FEET! CHICKEN FEET IN MY LOCKER. I DON'T EVEN KNOW the significance of this one. Or where you would even buy a ton of chicken feet. Or why the hell I haven't changed my locker combination.

I tie them up in an old Shakespeare paper and throw them away and spritz some perfume around my locker.

Try harder, Dykes.

I guess they got the message somehow, and I guess what's really stupid is that a dozen chicken feet in my locker bother me a lot less than *ETTA SINCLAIR IS A WHORE* scribbled on one of the whiteboards in calculus. What's extra stupid is that the dirty picture next to it looks like a really hideous drawing of (*some virgin's imagining of*—yeah, that's right, looking at you,

Natasha) cunnilingus, which is obviously the opposite of my crimes here. The Dykes probably couldn't bring themselves to form a penis with their perfect gold-star-lesbian hands.

Or maybe the Dykes didn't do it. Maybe this is Liliana or the girl from my gym class or someone else who found out the Dykes aren't guarding me anymore and it's duck season! Etta season! or something.

God, it's not even *creative*. And here's Tasha perched on the table chewing gum and giggling with seniors who would so not ever talk to some outcast junior except that she happens to be laughing at an outcast-outcast junior and so that makes it okay. As long as there's someone else below you, right, then you're fine.

It's times like this I miss Danielle. She'd be too busy messing around on her calculator figuring out equations that graph pornographically to give a shit about what was written about me on some board, and I guess that kind of stuff is the reason she got out of Saint Em's. And out of Nebraska.

I erase the board and the girls boo and throw colored pencils at my ass. Wow, Mr. Burbank, you can show up anytime now.

Natasha's the only one of the Dykes in this class. I don't know why that's making it harder, but it is, and I look at her and she looks back and I know that (a) she probably put that on the board; she's got this generic handwriting but she looks way too proud, and (b) even if she didn't, she's going to sit there and wish she did, and honestly that's just as bad. So the thing is that it isn't looking like some monolithic bullying force now, it's just *Natasha*. I used to walk her dog when she went out of town. I helped her brother build his tree house. I read *Twelfth Night* to her in dramatic inappropriate accents when we were stoned and cramming for our midterms last year. She's calling me a whore? Who's the one who asked me what sex was like? Who's the one who got all teary when she confessed to me she was a virgin, *tell me what it's like, you know so much about sex, Etta, tell me it's going to get better, you're so smart, Etta, you're so experienced.*

The goddamn bullshit of all of this, I swear. The whole world makes you think God forbid you actually enjoy sex, but at least you've got your friends to tell you all the right stuff about how a woman's sexual energy is no one's business but her own and should be respected, and that *Natasha, you shouldn't pretend to be more experienced than you are, being a virgin is nothing to be ashamed of.* (Being so incredibly desperate to lose your virginity and not having the balls to ask a girl out maybe is, but I didn't say that at the time and well I'm no longer friends with her, so way to be a brave one, there, Tasha.) *And, Etta, you are a paradigm of new waves of feminism blah blah blah,* but apparently new feminists are all lesbians, what do you know. I'm beginning to really wish Disco Dykes had come with a contract to sign or at the very least a memo. (The sad thing is I think I would have signed it, and I don't know what that says about me, and I really don't know what it says about the legitimacy of this sexuality I'm fighting so hard for.)

(Not gay enough, not straight enough, not sick enough, not healthy enough. I am Etta Not Otherwise Specified.)

(Or I'm Etta the bitch—written in rhinestone across my boobs and all—because I used to talk shit about Natasha behind her back, I'd bitch to Rachel that Tasha was obsessed with her and desperate and insecure and I'd make these little barbs to Natasha about her outfits because she was trying to horn in on my place with Rachel and *this is her revenge*.)

(Or. You know. I'm Etta the whore.)

Is it any wonder I cut class and go to the computer lab and commit the whole Brentwood site to memory?

"Mom?"

She looks up. She's in bed with her big work tray across her lap, looking through documents or something. She likes to make coffee and bring it back to her room and do work in her nightgown. I've always kind of loved that.

"Ettalou. What's wrong?"

"Can I sit with you?"

She moves her tray to the floor and fluffs up the comforter next to her. "Of course."

I crawl into bed next to her and rest my head on her shoulder. My mother is thin but soft, like she was supposed to be this way, like she doesn't care. She orders salads a lot. She orders them because she *likes salad*.

She turns her head to kiss my temple. "What's the matter?"

"Can I change schools?"

She sighs a little, but like she's sad, not like she's really exasperated with me. I wouldn't really blame her. We've had this conversation every time the Dykes and I have gotten into fights. Or anytime I've looked outside of our gay fantasy world and hated everyone else and looked back and hated us, too.

We pretended we were better than everyone.

The thing is that that's kind of gross.

"You're doing so well there," she says, then adds, "academically."

"It's really awful there, Mom."

"What happened?"

"Just this stupid fight." I hear myself making it sound smaller than it is, and I hate that, but I think I'm terrified that if I tell her the truth, she won't believe me. It will sound too big and too scary. *Bullying* is the subject of a TV movie. I don't fit that. Irony of irony, right? Here I am too small for something. (Or lying to myself to sound smaller, and isn't that more like me.) "All my stupid friends."

"Rachel too?"

"Sort of. Yeah."

She rubs circles on my back. "You two always work it out."

"But do we have to? I mean we keep saying I can ride this shit out but why should I *have* to?"

"Saint Emily's is going to do good things for you, sweetie. And just in retrospect, I know, and that really sucks. But a lot of people hate high school."

"It's . . . different."

"All those good colleges you want to go to? Saint Emily's is a great foot in the door. They're gonna see your grades at a tough school and give you a shot and then see you're just as amazing as that piece of paper makes you look."

"I just want to come before a piece of paper about me for once."

"You're the only person in the world who could pull that off, baby girl. God knows I couldn't. The system's not set up for personalities like yours, huh?"

"High school isn't set up for personalities like mine."

"Ha, that I can relate to."

"You hated high school?"

"With a passion. But I blocked it out and worked hard, and it helped me all the way to law school. I'd hate for a fight with your friends to ruin your future, wouldn't you?"

She's making it sound like I have some kind of say in what she decides. She's making it sound like she's deciding anything. She's not.

"Just public school, maybe?"

"Honey," she says. "Nothing in Nebraska's gonna make you happy."

"Screw Nebraska."

"Hey, if I'd known it would be this bad for you, I might have."

I've been telling her it's this bad for me since kindergarten. If she'd *believed* me, she might have gotten me out of here, and how damn frustrating is that for the girl who checked herself into therapy, you know?

"Year and a half, baby," she says. "Year and a half and you're out of here. Just ride it out, okay?"

Or I could get the hell out of here now.

"Okay," I say.

I need to get into Brentwood.

What I gathered from my Brentwood research is that I really need to learn how to sing. And I have chorus tomorrow, so all of a sudden everything's coming up Etta.

I have this fantasy that I'll just become a better singer, like this is *Legally Blonde* and this audition is my LSAT. I'll learn to sing on this drive to chorus, and then I'll get there and stun everyone. Word will get out and they'll move the audition forward just to accommodate my new talent. I'll sing and dazzle everyone, and that'll all be the first ten minutes of the show, and the rest of it will be me at Brentwood being awesome and having a tiny dog and whatever the hell else. I think she gets to slap her professor at one point, I'm not sure.

Unfortunately, half a run-through of the *In the Heights* sound track on my way to the community center is a billion times more than enough to teach me that *desperation* is clearly not one of the best methods toward improving your singing. So predictably I sound like shit all through chorus, and everyone looks at me even a little more like *why can't this black girl sing* than they usually do, so after rehearsal I suck it up and go up to Candice, our director, and I tell her about Brentwood and ask her if she knows how heavily singing is weighted for the audition, even though I was just on the website and guess how many sentences were devoted to telling you exactly what type and how much music you can bring in and whether or not you can expect an accompanist (four) and how many were even sort of about dancing (one half).

She's putting her music back into her folder. "Well," she says, "I can't say I'm all that familiar with Brentwood. They're a little too show-tuney for me!" Candice is very intense in her belief that no good music has been written after 1800. A *little too show-tuney for me!* might be a correct write-off in this case, but I've also been noticing lately that it's her critique of anything. Whenever I hold a note too long I'm being *a little too show-tuney for her!* If we want to try staggering the volume of the different sections through different parts of the song? A *little too show-tuney!* We think we should move rehearsal to Friday this week? A *little too show-tuney!*

I say, "But you know about this kind of program."

"As far as I know, musical theater programs do put a heavy stress on the musical portion rather than the theater."

"'Musical' should really include dancing. . . ."

"I think the consensus is that dancing, at least for a specific show, and acting, just in general, can be taught more readily than singing. Singing requires years and years of refinement."

"And a big heaping spoonful of natural talent." I've been taking voice lessons since I was a baby and I do not sound like Bianca, you can't fool me.

She says, "It's my opinion that with enough practice, anyone can get anywhere. Are you really passionate about improving, Etta? It can't just be to get into the program. You have to really want to sing better or you're going to get much too easily frustrated with the amount of work. And to really get your voice to its very peak takes years and years of continuous effort."

"I've been singing for ages."

"But to be a *singer*, you need to be highly disciplined."

It's the world's most triggering damn word, "discipline." I could have been four hundred damn pounds and laughed at every day, but I guarantee that if my weight had never gotten tied into the idea that I was a failure, that I didn't work hard enough, that I didn't *care* enough, I would be in my pointe shoes doing goddamn pas de chat right now.

I blink and look down.

"I'll be able to help you," Candice says. "If that's what you want."

I think about Bianca's tiny little body, her painful little

bones, but then I think about the notes falling out of her like they're nothing, and I think that there is something beautifully, fantastically unrestrained about it. I think that no amount of *discipline* is going to get me to the point where singing looks effortless.

And I think *what's the point, your mom's rich, stay in Nebraska until you graduate and then go to some nice school and stop whining about it.*

The problem is that if I don't go now, I'm scared I'm never going to go. What if I'm not really one of the people who's going to get out? What if I'm a delusional version of one of the people who stays?

"Thanks," I say. "I think I'm good."

I'm going to get there somehow.

9

"WHO ARE YOU TEEEEXTING."

"You're such a little kid, it's ridiculous."

Bianca bounces in front of my phone. "Who who who who."

"Maaaaason."

"Eeee!" She does a damn cartwheel. It's a bunch of days post-whiteboard-incident, so obviously it's been a bunch of texts, mostly from people I don't even know making dirty jokes (can't they just go back to talking behind my back instead of talking to my inbox?), but a good, beautiful handful of the texts are from Mason, and I'm supposed to see him tonight. He's texting me suggesting places. Dinner and a movie, what even is this? When did I sign up to date this boy? Whatever, I'm going with it.

Bianca and I are in one of the rooms on the fourth floor of the community center where a bunch of dance classes (but not my tap class, of course, because that would be too convenient) are taught. I'm pretty sure I did have a ballet class in this room at some point, when I was really young, but it's hard to tell because the whole damn building looks the same. But I think this might be off the hallway where Kristina had her hissy fit.

Anyway right now this room is empty and we came up here after group, since there's no audition prep today, to listen through some sound tracks and figure out what the hell I'm going to do for my audition. It's a little premature because, like Mason said, we don't sing our own choices unless we get through to the second audition, and it's also a little pointless because I still haven't figured out how to sing.

There's a piano in here, and Bianca cartwheels her way over to it and says, "Mason is singing 'Reviewing the Situation.' From *Oliver!*"

"Okay, that's pretty perfect."

"That's something you need," she says. "Something with a lot of *character*. That way if you're self-conscious about your voice you can act through it and half-talk and make that part of what you're doing. Not all songs need you to sing all pretty."

"Yeah, easy for you to say."

"It so is not, everything I sing sounds so *polished*. I can't be brassy and big. Even my 'Let's Hear It for the Boy,' which is—"

"Amazing."

"Okay, yeah, but it doesn't sound like how it's supposed to."

"That's what makes it interesting, and you totally know that's a good thing or you wouldn't sing it for every damn audition."

"I'm tryyyying to make you feel better."

"Usually chocolate is the answer for that."

She perks right up. "I'll buy you some!"

"I want to hear you sing."

"Noooo, we're supposed to be working on you."

"You sing. Then I will."

It doesn't take any more convincing than that, this goofy kid. Bianca jumps right up onto the piano and starts singing 'Reviewing the Situation,' which is this hilariously gritty song sung by this hilarious gritty guy, and she's right, it sounds about a hundred times prettier than it's supposed to be, but gaaawd it's hard to even imagine that that could be a problem when you're sitting on the floor of this studio and her voice is pouring on you like water. She's showing off now, grinning at me and making notes flutter in the back of her throat (notes that don't need to be held that long—*a little show-tuney for me!*) but she doesn't have to. This shy little thing (although not as shy with me anymore so much, and I'm beginning to think that maybe she was as desperate for friends as I was) sings like it's easier than talking.

I clap, and she bows and falls off the piano (no wonder this girl can't dance, she's this broken little doll) and says, "Now you!"

"I'm not singing 'Reviewing the Situation'!"

"Sing, um. What are you?"

"Short. Black. Awesome."

"Vocally!"

"I know I know. Mezzo-soprano. Who isn't?"

"Deep syrupy altos, that's who," she says, and she goes ahead and sings a few bars of 'Reviewing the Situation' down in the boy octave, and what even is this girl? Little. Blond. Gorgeous. A deep syrupy alto. "You like *Rent*, right? Even though it's, um, a white construction? Do 'Out Tonight.'"

"I can't do the high note in that, no way. Not a cappella at least."

She taps out a few notes on the piano, but she definitely doesn't know the music and even more definitely is no piano player. "Just do the intro," she says. "Stop at the part before she takes her clothes off."

"That doesn't sound like me." I'm really not ashamed of this. I'm really *not*, so screw you, Tasha.

"I'm gonna go home and *pray* for you."

"Bitch."

"Sing!"

So I do. I get up and wiggle around Mimi-style and sing about how she's gonna go slut around tonight, and the truth is that I'm kind of loving that Bee picked this song for me.

Rachel and I used to always listen to it when we got ready, flat-ironing her hair straight as a board and streaking on that white eye pencil and shrieking in my middle-of-nowhere bedroom that we were the felines of Avenue B.

I cut off before the high note, but Bianca just stands there (Bianca doesn't really sit, not when she can help it) and looks all delighted, and she says, "Etta, that was *so good!*" and I'm not complaining or anything, seriously, but this is the part where someone would normally compliment someone's voice, not just the performance, and she doesn't. Really, I'm not complaining. I'm not regretting that I sang or anything, I'm just saying that I feel like I let her down by not being secretly awesome.

God. Maybe I am regretting that I sang.

She says, "Hey, what? I said you were great."

"Clearly I'm not a good actor if I'm coming across all disappointed."

"Aw, hey, Etta . . ."

"No no no, I'm sorry."

"I kind of thought you were going to be really bad," she says. "I mean, just the way you talk about yourself. I was sort of wondering. You're so incredibly far from bad."

"I know that! I never said I was awful. I'm just, you know, not a singer. And you have to be a singer for this audition. It's okay."

She shakes her head. "You're better than I thought, but I still stand by my earlier, um, prescription. Something with character. So you can dance like you just did."

"Whaaa?"

"Like you just did?"

"No no no, sweetie, that wasn't dancing, that was being a whore. Good God, what do they teach in church nowadays? Aren't you supposed to be able to pick whores out of a lineup?"

"That's only on Sundays," she says. "It's Thursday, my secret Christian Whore-Spotting Powers aren't activated."

"I can't dance in my audition," I say. "Not in the singing part, anyway. Like, could I make it any more obvious that I'm using my dancing as a crutch? Nuh-uh."

She scrambles to the boom box she brought and starts rooting through CDs. "Wait wait wait."

"And this is all kind of moot and ridiculous because we have just proved that I'm not good enough at singing a song *without* character to get through to second round, and with my luck they'll pick, like . . . 'Till There Was You.'"

"Did I or did I not say *wait wait wait?*"

"Yeah but I was mid-monologue already."

She says, "You know *A Chorus Line*, right?"

"Not really. I saw the movie like ten years ago, and it's burned in my brain with how horrible it is."

"Oh Gosh no do not even *talk* to me about the movie. Whoever put that on screen should be . . . I can't think of a suitable punishment for letting that move be made. Tied down and forced to watch it."

"The actual show's better?"

"The actual show is . . . Well, the actual *music* is incredible. And this song is so you, I can't even believe it, listen listen."

So I listen listen. It's this brassy-voiced woman sing-talking her way through an explanation of her father treating her like shit, and then she went to the ballet and it showed her this world where men were chivalrous and perfect and . . . and goddamn it, Bianca.

She says, "You could even sing it more than she does. You could let yourself break through on the high . . . Are you okay?"

"I just want to listen."

When the first singer is finished and a second starts, Bianca pushes pause. "And then the two other girls sing. But that part is Sheila's all to herself, and I think . . . you know?"

I swallow over and over and over. "I know."

Full, honest disclosure: I'm not really the girl with daddy issues.

When my parents got divorced, I was six, and my mom immediately brought me and Kristina to this kids' counselor so we could work through our feelings. I think Mom read something about if you don't deal with these things right away they escalate and then your daughters end up freaking out and getting eating disorders or something, I don't know.

So off we went to mold Play-Doh and draw pictures and talk about our feelings, and I don't remember my dad even coming up that often. Our counselor gave us candy when we cried, so we used to pinch each other under the table (Kristina's idea).

Anyway, the truth about the whole eating disorder thing is that I really don't see what the hell it has to do with my dad, probably because the thing with my dad is just so *stupid*. He pays his child support when he's supposed to but he never wants to see us and he lives like *right here*, two blocks away from the community center. I guess at some point I should have some dramatic confrontation with him. I should appear on his doorstep and sing "At the Ballet" as a symbol of how ballet was my only savior from this horrible fatherless life that he gave me, and I guess maybe that's what Bianca thinks is going on here. And the truth is that's really, really not what's going on here, because I didn't have a horrible fatherless life, I just had an ordinary, stable, happens-to-be-fatherless life.

But I guess I know these issues because I guess everyone's been waiting for me to develop them, and everyone's expecting me to start crying in group and talking about how my father is the root of all my issues, so I guess I'm saying that I can act this out pretty well.

I guess I'm saying that when I'm on my way to meet Mason singing along to the CD, playing Shelia's part over and over again, there's really no reason for me to be crying.

Or maybe I'm saying that I'm not crying because I'm picturing my father.

I'm picturing *The Nutcracker*.

10

I RECOUNT SOME OF THIS TO MASON, SOME WATERED-DOWN
version that doesn't include me crying over show tunes (not so
much because I think he would judge me but because I think
that the fact that I'm whatevermaybekindofdating someone
who wouldn't judge me is some kind of miraculous bubble
I don't want to burst), and he says, "So I don't get it, why did
you stop dancing?"

Okay, so this I *really* don't feel like getting into. I've spilled
my guts about this once this week, that's really enough. "I still
dance. I do tap and modern and I did ballroom over the summer. I just don't do ballet."

"Which was your favorite."

"Favorite isn't exactly . . . the term."

"So what is?"

There's no word for the thing that makes you lose your damn breath every time you get up on your toes.

"I don't know." Subject change! "So what's the thing for you, that, you know, crux. Singing?"

"Eh, I like acting better than singing anyway, but no, none of that really."

"I hope you tell them this at your audition!"

He laughs. "I'm not making it far in this audition. I'm just doing it for James and James is just doing it for Bianca. It's all this big . . . I'm not complaining, you know, I love the girl, but it feels all the time that we're making this little dream world for Bianca. Like a house made out of candy. Shitty metaphor but whatever."

"Right."

"I don't know. We do things to make her feel safe. And she needs it, it's fine. But it does kind of require this—well, you know, song and dance of getting amped to go to a theater school that . . . I mean, don't get me wrong, I'd love it, but I'm not good enough and there are other people who'd love it more. Like Bianca. And you, maybe."

I shrug. "I used to apply every year just for . . . you know, the hell of it. Like talking to mall Santas when you're a kid. You know, just in case *this* one's the real Santa."

"Oh, God, right?"

"Like crossing your fingers every time. Getting the photo taken. Your mom fluttering by because she's afraid he'll cop a feel."

"Seriously?"

"Being a girl, man, there's some weird shit."

He says, "But you do want to go, right?"

"You know what? I want Bianca to go. Give me some powdered sugar to decorate the candy-house walls, I guess."

He laughs and says, "We don't know how many people are getting in. Could be both of you."

"Anyone who tried to justify admitting both of us is obviously deaf in one ear and Bianca and I are singing in different ones. Me in the deaf one, if that wasn't clear."

"I bet you can sing."

"I just am so incredibly not in her league."

"No one is."

"Yeah. I don't know why we're trying with these auditions when she's our competition."

He sips his drink and thinks. "Because she's miserable."

It kind of works as an answer.

"Okay then," I say. "So what's your dream?"

"I want to be a biologist. Or a basketball player. I want to be a basketball player who does biology on the side."

"Obviously, because that's the one of the two that makes the more reasonable career."

"Obviously."

"Looking at schools?"

"I don't really have the grades right now, is the thing. I'm thinking I'm going to stay here and do community college for a while, and then we'll see what happens. Maybe I'll pull myself up by my bootstraps and everyone will be inspired and just give me things."

"That's the dream, right?"

"I think so."

I'm enjoying this. I haven't had a good conversation with a boy in a long time, and yeah, maybe this is a little on the bantery side of things, but it's nice, we're not bored, we're smiling at each other, and, yeah, he's really cute. I don't think anything's going to come of this, though, and I really, really hope that doesn't mess things up with James and Bianca. The thing is that I don't know anything about biology and he doesn't know anything about . . . I don't know, there's got to be something I care about. Lesbians. I don't know.

Okay, the thing is that he just said the words "turned off," and I dried up like an old frog.

Someone kicks my chair leg, hard, as she walks by, and I turn around and yep, that's Clara, some sophomore. Awesome. Now it—and I don't know what *it* is, but it's enough to make me squirm down to my stomach—is happening outside of school too. I guess I'm surprised it took this long. Small school, small town.

I guess some of me is surprised that it happened at all, and doesn't that just suck.

"You okay?" Mason says, and I can tell that he saw me jump but didn't see the kick.

"Fine. You're really okay with staying in Nebraska?"

"Ugh, did I really give that impression?"

"Community college, not gunning for Brentwood . . ."

"Hey, neither are you, you're just gunning for *anywhere but here*."

"Yeah, fair."

"Look," he says. "At the end of the day, there's people who are staying and people who are going, and trust me, I know a fair number of each, and neither of us has a drop of *staying* in our damn blood."

I wonder which Bianca is. I know which Rachel is. I know which Danielle was. "I guess I'm pretty transparent," I say.

"Eh. I like you."

"So, what if we don't get out? What if we're these people made to get out and we *don't*?"

"We explode or become alcoholics. How's your food?"

How's your food.

People don't ask me this. People count out my calories to make sure I'm eating. My mom watches me pour my six ounces of whole milk with every meal. My sister counts cookies to make sure two are missing. My mom stops herself in the middle of commenting on everything I eat—*are you really— what? Nothing, dear!*

But no one asks me how my food *is*. I mean, it's delicious, this is a nice place, whatever. But now I'm staring down at it and I can't even figure out what it is. I can't taste it anymore.

I can't remember it. I can't even make out the shapes of it. It's transmogrified itself into *FOOD*. It's like what they ate in *The Sims*. It's a plate of *FOOD*.

I'm eating *FOOD*.

I'm sitting here eating it.

Shit.

This was a mistake. The date. Not eating. Eating. Letting him know my history. Letting him think I'm over it. Ordering this. Ordering anything. This was a mistake.

God, what the hell is wrong with me. It's just a *question*. What the hell am I going to do if anyone ever comments on my actual weight? I've gained a shit-ton in the past few months, am I really telling myself that no one important is ever going to mention that? That no one's *noticed*? I go to a freaking all-girls school, how long is it going to be before someone says something and fragile little Etta just breaks into fragile damn pieces? How long do I have to do this before I figure out that being this shatterable thing *isn't fucking cute*?

They've all noticed. They've all been looking at me and thinking I'm enormous and whispering to each other not to say anything.

The people in this restaurant are looking at me.

They're counting my calories.

Not in a good way.

I take a deep breath, feel it fill me, fill me all the way up. Set my fork down.

"It's good," I say. "Thank you."

"Course. So did you and Bianca talk about what you're going to sing . . . ?" And I have no idea what the rest of the conversation is about.

By the time he drops me off he's figured out that something's up. He asked me a few times and I blew him off, and people have a couple of different reactions to that, I've learned in my charming history of blowing people off, and he's one of the ones who get pissed. I like that better than self-deprecating and depressed, like Ben, so there's that.

Which isn't to say I don't feel shitty about this.

"I'm sorry," I say. "It's not you."

"I must have said something."

"No, seriously. I just get all up in my head about stuff."

He unlocks my door. "You think too much."

"What?"

"That's, like, my diagnosis. You think too much."

He kisses me and walks me to my door and I'm inside before I figure out what it was about that that really bothered me—I can't get a freaking doctor to diagnose me, and I go out on one date with a guy and *he thinks he can*?

I'm upstairs, breathing hard, on my phone.

"Rachel. It's me."

Goddamn it.

"It's Etta, I need to talk to someone. It rang before it

went to voice mail, I know your phone's on, Ray. . . ."

Goddamn it.

"Can we just, can we put whatever this is on hold, I just . . . I r-really need someone to talk to, I just completely zombied my way through a whole"—date—"conversation because someone asked me a totally normal-person question and I think I'm slipping hard and I need you, okay—" And goddamn if Kristina hears me I'm so completely screwed and she's going to cry herself to sleep again, I need to be *fine* for her (I need to be a good role model, need to be perfect-skinnyGodno), and I cannot call Bianca with this, I cannot call skinny little I-win-at-eating-disorders Bianca because Bianca never would have *ordered FOOD* what was I thinking shit shit shit.

"Rachel, please . . ."

Nothing.

I hang up. Call again. Nothing.

Okay. Okay. Okay.

I don't know what else to do, so I call Bianca, and trust me, I hate myself for it, I really do, because she does not need this dumped on her, I haven't seen her eat a damn bite since she had that salad over a week ago, and obviously she's had something since then, everyone eats, I remember that finding out that even real anorexics have to eat *something* was this horrible epiphany when I was eleven, like finding out fairies weren't real, so she must have eaten something but I don't have any proof and I guess I'm believing in fairies again, whatever, but I can't put this on her. I really just can't. So why the hell am I calling her.

Stay classy, Etta.

"Hello?"

It's not Bianca.

I cling to that, to the fact that somehow fate has saved Bianca from this shit, before I even process that this is not the person I wanted to call and now I'm about to cry on the phone to who knows who.

"Etta? Hey hey hey what's wrong?" It's enough words for me to recognize the voice.

"J-James?"

"Hey, yeah."

"Where's Bianca, is she okay?"

"Yeah, yeah, she's fine. She's stranded at the kitchen table right now, I'm waiting up here."

"What?"

"My parents won't let her get up until she finishes a hamburger. She's been there a few hours."

"God."

"I was with her for a while but eventually she wanted me to leave. So . . . here I am."

"My family doesn't think I'm sick." That's not fair, really. I don't know what Kristina thinks. We really, really don't talk about it.

But I have to say something right now, and apparently that something is ascribing issues to myself like I just got mad at Mason for doing to me. God, I really do think too much. I didn't disagree with *that*.

James says, "Yeah, ours didn't think so for a long time either."

"Can she eat it?"

He's quiet for too long. It's like the pause when one reporter switches to another and there's that delay when you wait for the second one to realize that it's their turn. Now back to you, James.

"No," he says. "I don't think she can."

And . . . I know I don't look like it. I'm really aware that I don't look like it. And I know it's not the case now, and that I'm doing, comparatively, really really well. But for some reason that's making me think now that I was never mentally where she is, and I so was. In July the Dykes got me an ice cream cake for my birthday and they knew it would be hard for me, they weren't stupid, but they cut me this tiny slice and put it in front of me and said *it's your birthday, Etta, you can give yourself a break on your birthday, right?* and it was mint chocolate chip and it looked so good and I wanted it so much and that was the thing, I *wanted* it. It wasn't a matter of not wanting to eat anymore. It wasn't a matter of pretending I wasn't hungry. I couldn't do it. I put a bit into my mouth and it melted and it tasted so good and I spit it out. I couldn't do it.

I couldn't swallow. I stared at that piece-minus-one-bite until it was brown and green sludge.

Just because I could eat it now, just because Bianca is still there, I feel like I never was.

It's the opposite of when you're there, when you're entrenched in it, and you exaggerate to yourself how deep in it you are, how sick you are, when you tell yourself you have the best little eating disorder in the world because it's the only thing that keeps you from ripping out your skin to pull out your bones and weigh them. And then you're out of it and you think, *I must have been imagining it, I couldn't have been that bad, if I were really that bad then someone would have stopped me.*

Someone would have sat me down and made me eat and *worried* about me. They wouldn't have been pissed because I was wasting their damn ice cream cake.

And that's it. I'm crying.

"Hey hey hey, all right." James's voice is deeper, suddenly, gentler. "All right, Etta. We're all right."

"I'm sorry. Please don't tell her I called. Shit."

"Slow down. Tell me what happened."

"I was on a freaking . . . date, a *dinner* date, with Mason, and then he just . . . he mentioned the food and—"

"Did he say something?"

"He didn't do anything wrong, it was so normal and stupid and . . ."

"And you're upset."

"I don't know what I think gives me any right to be around normal people."

"You're not that weird, Etta."

"No, I think I'm pretty weird."

"Why?"

Why.

Huh.

"Because I'm gay. Sort of. Um. Not. Half of me is gay."

"That's really not going to win you any weird points with me."

"Because I'm messed up about food."

"Have you seen who I live with?"

"Because all my friends hate me?"

"You're really grasping at straws, here."

"Uh. Broken home? Racial minority? Short?" I'm obviously screwing around now (and calming down, this is working) but there is an answer here, there is *something*. There is something really fundamentally wrong with me, something that's keeping me from connecting with people the way that I'm supposed to. It's like all this stuff I try to fix about myself, all of these problems that I say I have, are just me trying to represent, trying to *justify* this weird broken part of me that nobody else is seeing. "There's something *bad* in me," I say. "There's something about me that's clearly just . . ."

"Why?" he says. "Why's it clear?"

"Because if I were normal, I would feel bad about this shit

that I do and the way that I hurt people and I would be actually upset about what people at school are doing to me but, but I'm *not*. I would feel bad about the fact that I lost all of my friends, but I don't, I don't feel *anything*. I don't *feel* anything. And at least when I wasn't eating I felt *hungry*. . . ."

"Until you didn't," James says. "Until you didn't feel anything."

"I don't know."

"Etta. Honey. This recovery thing, this is new still."

"There's something wrong with me."

"Etta."

"Normal people can't put themselves through what I did and just *be okay*. I'm supposed to still be suffering. I'm not supposed to be able to get better because that means it was *never that bad*."

"No, it doesn't. It means that you're the most self-motivated, self-sufficient person I've ever even heard of. You're a . . . well, you're a really good influence for my little sister, I'll tell you that."

"I am?"

"Maybe you haven't noticed, but I'm pretty damn protective of her."

"What? News to me."

"Shut up."

I flop onto my bed and squeeze my eyes shut. I am suddenly so, so tired.

"I just want to respond to something in a normal way," I say. "Just one damn time. I want to relate to someone at the time I'm supposed to be relating to them."

"You just wish that you'd jumped off your cliff at the same time as someone else," he says.

I nod. I feel like he can see it.

"You don't have to feel guilty that you suffered alone," he says. "That's not how this works. You don't have to apologize to us because you were unhappy."

"Okay."

"And you don't have to apologize for being okay without us."

"But . . ." I want to need someone.

"Hey," he says. "I'm not hanging up."

"Okay. Yeah. Okay."

"Okay."

I'm listening over and over to the first minute-thirty of "At the Ballet" when I click over to Facebook. I haven't been on in a few days because it's depressing to see the Dykes posting pictures of themselves going out, lip gloss, kissy faces, dark-circle-smudged mascara to prove it's been a good night (at least Rachel doesn't have Facebook, she's pretty committed to the seventies thing). And it's depressing to see Ben with his new girlfriend, even though I don't technically care, and, even more depressing, Danielle smiling behind coffee cups and I'm wondering like a damn creeper who's taking these pictures and if she's really single like her page says and why we're still friends. (Because we still like each other. Because we promised to stay friends. Which, obviously, explains why I haven't texted her and I didn't answer, a week after the breakup, when she texted me. I don't know why. I protect myself and sabotage myself at the worst times.)

I have a hundred thousand notifications, and I click and see they're all for the same thing—Etta Sinclair was tagged in a picture, twenty-six people liked a picture of you, eighteen comments on a picture of you . . . Natasha Metrovsky posted a picture of you.

I'm thinking it's some ugly outtake of a Rachel's bathroom photo shoot and how bad could it really be until I click and shit, that's a Photoshopped picture of me with a dick in my mouth, and it was Photoshopped well because Natasha has no life outside of buying bell-bottoms and faking hookups and stealing *my best friend* (who doesn't have Facebook, who hasn't liked the picture, who hasn't seen the picture, who had nothing to do with this, Rachel Rachel Rachel) and here are people from Saint Em's that I've never talked to, goddamn seniors, goddamn *freshmen*, laughing at me for taking this picture and *what a stupid whore* and Natasha's *I know, right, what a slut*, and who are these freaking *guys* going *lol look at that fat bitch, guy must have been desperate* and my *baby sister* commenting defending me and saying it's not real when how the hell could she even be sure and oh my God, oh my God, oh my God.

It's hard to practice singing when you're crying this hard but I do it anyway because I freaking have to get out of Nebraska and if this is a chance I will take it, I will take anything. I'm feeling it, okay? I'm *feeling this shit,* okay? Get me *out.*

11

OUR FIRST AUDITION IS IN BELLEVUE, WHERE I HAVEN'T BEEN since the ballet company I was in before BN, a long time ago. I don't want to drive that far, and James has never been there (who the hell has never been to Bellevue?) and it's not like Mason can fit us all on his motorcycle so it's public transportation for us! Bianca's paranoid of being late so we're on it crazy early, seven forty-five on a Saturday, which at least means it's practically empty. Bianca yawns and folds up onto her seat and goes to sleep (I'm not sure I've ever seen her sit, she stands or she perches like she's about to jump up or she collapses into these helpless little heaps) and James nudges his backpack under her head and plays with her wrist, and Mason and I swing from the bars and sing "Santa Fe" and make Bianca smile in her sleep.

Please let me get through. Please let me get to a second audition.

Honestly, for a second I think I don't want to get in as much as I want *this* to never stop.

There's no one from my school on this bus. There's just my little group of show-tuney people. Mason tugs me into his waist and sings the romantic part (so much as it is) of "Santa Fe" to me, and I laugh with my head tipped back and feel pretty. He picks me up like it's nothing, my legs around his waist, and swings me around. "Ugh, so heavy," he whispers, just to me, so obviously a joke, and I kick his back with my shoes and I *like* it, I like that joke, I like that he's so much taller and stronger than me that it's actually a joke, and I like myself so much for taking that joke. He just called me heavy and made me like myself. I didn't overthink it! How about that.

I kiss him, and he whispers, "Beautiful."

Other people start boarding eventually, but none of them are from my school so me and Mason don't really give a shit, we keep singing and dancing (or whatever Mason calls what he's doing. How the hell did these people get through fifteen years of musical theater training without learning how to do a fox-trot?) and Bianca's awake now and embarrassed and blushing into her sleeves but that's better than letting her worry herself sick about the audition, so I keep being loud and obnoxious and I get down on one knee and sing all of "Memory" to a twelve-year-old boy until Bianca's switched from screeching

"Ettaaaaaa!" in horror to just cringing and ducking into her collar, and then I go up and squish between her and James and wrap my arms around her. "I'm sorrrry."

She leans against me. "You're horrible."

"This is how people get famous! Being horrible in public! How are you going to get famous sitting here all quiet, huh?"

"Who says I want to get famous?"

"These people, look at 'em, every single one of them knows I can do a kind of acceptable rendition of 'Memory.' They have no idea how good *you* are!"

"I don't want them to!"

"Now that doesn't make any sense," Mason says, so I don't have to, thanks, kid. "You always say all you want to do with your life is sing. Don't sing on the bus if you don't want to, but don't give Etta any crap about not wanting to do this when you grow up either."

She shakes her head. "I don't, I don't."

But I have no time to comment on that because the bus pulls over at the next stop, and who should board but Isabel, Natasha, Titania, Rachel. All four of them.

"Dykes," I whisper urgently, as they're showing the bus driver their IDs with those practiced *we are totally humoring you by showing you our IDs because we are so much better than you that you shouldn't be allowed to ask us anything, hair flip* expressions. I shift James's backpack and shrink down behind it. "Dykes. Dykes. Dykes."

"Did they see you?" Bianca whispers back.

"I don't know. Probably. They have crazy gay X-ray vision."

"X-gay vision," James says, just to be a dick, but he makes me laugh and I *hear* them stop showing the bus driver their IDs, and yep, crazy gay high-frequency hearing. I'm screwed.

I don't know what they're going to do, but I know that I'm not expecting it when they go sit down a few rows ahead of us all innocuously and start groaning about how tired they are. I guess they were out all night and are too hungover to drive. They're wrung out, wrinkled, sweaty, and Farrah-haired and white-sunglassed, limp and glamorous like tie-dye with the colors squeezed out.

"God, that girl Marie would not get off me last night," Titania says, rolling her neck around until it cracks.

Natasha says, "She is so obsessed with you, I swear. But who could blame her, with those shoes." That's really weird, why is Natasha sucking up to Titania?

"Such cute shoes," Rachel says, and yeah, all right, that's messed up, because I know (a) shoes and (b) Rachel and those shoes are (c) hideous so she is (d) faking. So seriously, what ? Rachel's not queen bee anymore?

Did I do that?

(I'm not stupid. A part of me — a big part of me — knew that a lot of this shove-Etta-out bullshit had nothing to do with my rogue heterosexual ways and was just Isabel, Natasha, and Titania being opportunistic about shoving me out. They were

never my friends as much as we were all Rachel's, no matter what little anecdotes I can pull out, and it was so obvious that they wanted me out, that I was the thing between
them and moving up a rank in our whatever, because I don't
know, they were planning to put Disco Dykes on their tran-
scripts, or because maybe they're the same status-obsessed
female-stomping wannabes they always say are a symptom
of the heterosexual patriarchy. I'm just saying, it's funny that
Natasha did this whole paper last semester on how all subjugation of women at the hands of women is all actually because of
guys and here they are using me sleeping with a guy as a nice
convenient medium through which they can be dicks to me.
Who's driving who, here, Miss Daisy?)

Anyway the Dykes keep chattering away—though not so
much Rachel—about who they hooked up with (lying) and
who they wish they'd hooked up with (understating) and who
was there and who wasn't and what they're going to do tonight
and oh my God *drinkiiing! Tina Turnerrrrr!* and I can't figure
out why the hell they're not being mean to me until it hits me
like a damn brick. They think they're making me jealous.

They think I'm sitting here wishing I were with them.
They think I'm kicking myself for heading to an audition
instead of creeping onto a bus at eight thirty after what I know
from experience, lately, was a really disappointing club crawl.

The fact that I used to want to do this—that I used to
really, genuinely love these girls, because they didn't have to

be my friends, I didn't even have to like them, because they were my *family*—makes something still feel a little uneasy in me, but I say *go away uneasiness* and I lean my head back and smile and rest my cheek on Bianca's shoulder. "Brave," she whispers to me.

When I open my eyes, Rachel—just Rachel—is watching me. I smile at her a little.

She smiles back.

On the way into the high school where the auditions are, this boy I don't know, this boy from *Bellevue*, says, "Hey, Etta Sinclair! Want a hand?"

Bianca whispers, "What's he talking about?"

I rush her forward. "Never mind, sweetpea. Keep walking. Everything's fine."

12

WE WALK THROUGH THE FRONT DOORS OF THE HIGH SCHOOL—
marked with just this one poster, BRENTWOOD AUDITIONS, OPEN,
10 A.M.–2 P.M.—and it's like Dorothy stepping into Oz. All of
a sudden we're not in brown little Bellevue anymore with its
awful guys. (I have chosen to believe that all Bellevue boys are
as terrible as that one because I am mad, and if the Dykes at
their all-girls school can decide that they'll never be attracted
to a guy, I can make sweeping generalizations too, damn it.)
We're in this mess of hallways that probably looks way more
normal in its real life (though public school buildings will
always be just so eighties' movies to me) but are now crawling
with glitter and music and girls melting down by the bath-
rooms. There are roughly five hundred million times more
people here than I was expecting. Which I guess isn't saying all

that much given that I'm obviously exaggerating but also given that for some reason I'd narrowed the auditionees down in my head to just me, Mason, James, and Bianca. Never mind the thirty other people we've been meeting with a couple times a week. Never mind that all of eastern Nebraska is here and not just tiny little Schuyler. I guess in my head I hadn't pictured central Nebraska high school high-powered theater geeks as so bountiful but man, if I were shopping for the precious few Midwestern gay boys I would be all over this shit. The ones inside here are all okay. The ones inside can stay.

Which probably explains the look on James's face right about now.

"Go talk to him," Bianca whispers to him.

He startles. "What?"

She swallows and nods to the corner. "The tall one, blue hair? That's the one?"

"Bee . . ."

"It's just talking, right? We're allowed to talk. Ask him if he's nervous." She twists the hem of her shirt in her hands.

"Are you . . . Okay. Stay with Etta."

"I'm not five."

He kisses the top of her head and gives this imploring look to Mason, who rolls his eyes and goes with him. Wingman! I like them. I like them most together.

"Oh my gosh I'm so nervous," she says.

"Hey, hey, what? No no no, you're supposed to be the old

pro talking me down here." Because Jesus Christ, when was the last time I was at an audition, day camp? There are so many people, and they're muttering to themselves and practicing steps on the floor and singing scales with their eyes scrunched shut and . . . holy shit.

"How many people are going through?" she says.

"Don't ask me things like I'm supposed to know them!"

"Why does that girl have sheet music? I thought we didn't need sheet music!"

"Damn it, Bee!"

"Hhhhhoh my Gosh. I need to sit down."

"Hey, hey, yeah." I sit her down on the floor and find a granola bar in my pocket and break off half so it will be less intimidating. "Have you had anything today?"

She shakes her head.

"Eat that. I mean it."

She nods and starts nibbling. Good girl.

I go over to check with the people in charge and find out that we don't need sheet music, some people are just annoying and come over-prepared to mess with the rest of our heads, apparently, that we're going to be split up boys-girls and called in groups of ten that correspond to our numbers — here are your numbers, yay, Bianca and me together — and that until then we should sit and wait and blah blah blah also I make it a point to drift awkwardly close to Mason and James and Gay Boy and discover Gay Boy's name is Ian and make

James-Ian babies in my head all the way back to Bianca.

"Do you want ninety-one or ninety-two?" I say.

She looks at me like it's a trick question. I hold up the papers with our numbers on them. "Two," she says.

"A noble choice." I tape it to her chest for her.

"Where's Jamie?"

"Talking to that boy still, look."

"Does he have his number?"

"Not yet." Which is less noteworthy, if you ask me, than the fact that he hasn't come back to check on Bianca. It's not really a secret whether nailing the audition or keeping an eye on his sister is his real priority here.

At least, it isn't to me.

Bianca?

"What if they don't let him in?" she says.

"Hey, he'll get his number. He's with Mason, you know he's on top of shit."

"Right . . ."

"Hey. Look at me."

She looks at me.

"We've got this, okay? We've been practicing our asses off. And this is nothing. Sing a few lines, dance in a big group for a minute and a half? Whatever. Just smile and hit your notes and you'll sail through no problem. Ew, not that smile. Come on. Real smile. There you go."

"What are we singing?"

I scan the paperwork they gave me. "I don't know. I guess it's a surprise. Here, fill this out."

I watch her writing down her ton of experience like she's done it a hundred times, because she has done it a hundred times (hence ton of experience), and I write down all my dance classes and feel like a liar because I haven't done modern in forever and I still haven't dug my toe shoes out of the backyard and why did I just say "still" when I'm not going to, I don't *need* to, this is not a ballet school, I am not a ballerina, I need to be a musical theater kid to get through this so I will be a musical theater kid, but it can't hurt, I guess, so I write it all down and then write down chorus and musical theater day camp in small letters like that will make them not ask me to sing or something. Dream big, Etta.

"Look," I say. "The boys are getting their numbers. Everything's fine."

"Did you talk to the boy?"

"No, I just walked awkwardly close to them so I could eavesdrop a little. Sounds like his name's Ian."

"He's cute."

"Uh-huh."

"Does James like him?"

"I don't know, boo."

"I hope so," she says, but she sounds like she isn't sure, and how is it so easy to forgive her for that when I still want to punch my mom every time she clears her throat and changes the subject? Bianca's *trying*. She told James to talk to him. She's keeping this secret from her parents. I mean, hell, she's friends with me.

I rest my head on her shoulder. "I know."

They call us in group by group, alternating boys and girls, and by the time they get to us I'm a total stress case from waiting so long. Meanwhile, Bianca's cooled completely off, stepped into this confidence costume, and is smiling at the auditioners and politely at the other girls in our group and scuffling her feet casually while we get into our lines. Seeing her in the context of all these other girls makes me realize kind of anew how ridiculously tiny she is. What were the Dykes thinking when they saw me with her? You can't *not* notice that. It's impossible to ignore. I'm suddenly all worried about doing the dance combination, that she'll fall and hurt herself.

I need to calm down about her.

I think I'm going down a bad road here.

Dancing's first. They teach us this really easy combination—I'm talking largely grapevines and box steps, like, stuff I was doing while I was in Pull-Ups—and most people seem to have it all right. There are a few other dancers in the group, but really I can only tell because they hold themselves differently, because no one's tripping over their feet doing this. And . . . it kind of sucks, honestly. Really my only hope was that they'd try to teach us this ridiculously hard dance and everyone else would fall over and break their ankles and I would dazzle them all and tada instant scholarship. Ah well. Bianca's actually on the lower end of the spectrum here, but she's not awful. I'm probably the only one who can tell she's a little off. Well. Me and the two women auditioning us. Point your toes, Bee!

I hiss it into her ear during a turn, and she does. Good girl.

We run through it a few times as a group, then line by line. It feels nice, moving around at the same time as people to something besides tap, but yeah, this isn't really dancing. Still, one of the women auditioning us, the one with the clipboard, is watching me really closely, and I see her nod a little and make a note. That's got to be a good sign.

I'm extra convinced that that was a good note when she makes the same face when Bianca starts singing—okay, maybe a little more of a smile for Bianca than for me, but that's pretty understandable. We're singing "Far from the Home I Love," from *Fiddler*, which seems like a kind of bizarre choice, but I'm going with it. The girl next to me is freaking out, whispering, "Why couldn't they have chosen something from *Spring Awakening*?" which is such a weird musical to expect to show up at an audition. Seriously, it was on Broadway for like six minutes and it's about German teenagers having sex. *Fiddler on the Roof* at least has zillions of years of history behind it, even if "Far from the Home I Love" is a really dreary song. I mean, it's pretty, but it's not the kind of a song a girl without a great voice is going to be able to act her way through.

Well. Not without some serious effort. And do I look like Etta "Halfass" Sinclair to you? No, I'm Etta "Kick It in the Ass" Sinclair. I'll make this work.

But first Bianca, and the auditioner who loves her, and yeah, she's amazing. The accompanist is beaming at her when she's done, and the other girls are looking at her like they want to roast her on a spit. Bianca gives everyone this polite little smile on the way back to her seat and gives me the world's most subtle high five.

My turn. I stand up by the piano and take a second to close my eyes and get into character before I nod at the accompanist. And then I'm there. I don't think about the music—I know this song, I used to put shirts on my head and do "Matchmaker, Matchmaker" with my sister when I was little, I know *Fiddler*. I just tell myself I'm in love with this gorgeous guy and he has to go live in Siberia and that really sucks but what the hell because I love him and he loves me and nothing else matters. Everyone else did it all sad and mournful, so I go the other way. I close my eyes sometimes, I smile a little, because I am so willing to move to Siberia for this boy. I'm excited about loving someone enough to go to Siberia. I'm brave and strong and *bring me to New York, auditioners*. It's totally a bad metaphor because Nebraska itself is about as *far from the home I love* as anything could ever be, but right now I'm singing and pretending how much I would miss this place if I left. I'm thinking about the gross movie theater with the stale popcorn and the weird farmers' restaurant and the retro coffee shop and Rachel Rachel Rachel and then I think about New York and bright lights and bigger things and all these *feelings* come out of nowhere, maybe my sister could visit me at school someday, maybe me and Bianca could be roommates, I am so willing to make this leap of goddamn faith, everything I love, all these freaking feelings, all the phone numbers of these new friends and all the beautiful people I could meet, they are all coming with me. I do not need to be here. I can be as far from the home I don't love as is physically possible.

And then the song's over and clipboard lady says, "Thank you," and everything rushes out. The other girls are looking at me like I totally screwed this up.

I think I did okay.

"Callbacks will be posted online by the end of the week," they tell us.

"How'd it go?" we ask the boys after.

Mason shrugs. James keeps talking to Ian.

Called back:

Bianca Grey
James Grey
Ian O'Donnell
a bunch of people we don't care about
Me

13

"SO ARE YOU OKAY?" I ASK.

"Yeah." He plays with his straw, letting it fill with coffee, capping it with his finger, tapping the coffee out, filling it up again. "Yeah, I'll be fine. More time for basketball and stuff. And I can pull some more shifts, I wanted to save up and fix the paint on my bike anyway. It's all scratched up around the tires."

"Stupid roads," I say.

"Seriously. How dare they."

I do believe that Mason will be okay, but I also believe that he's sad. I think maybe he wasn't taking it seriously because he thought he didn't have to, that he could get a second audition in his sleep. He did it before.

I so want to ask him what happened, if he fell, if he missed a note, if he just didn't stand out enough. I guess I'm trying to figure out why I got through, and even though I have literally no reason to think that he might be thinking the same thing—he's been nothing but happy and supportive of me, hasn't shown any sign that he thinks I don't deserve it—I'm convinced that he's sitting here wondering why the hell I got through and he didn't. Because frankly this is kind of ridiculous. I've always been a fan of musical theater, but I never really thought of myself as someone who was actually involved in it. It's like that season of *Survivor* when they brought fans in to play against people who'd been on the show before. I just went from sitting on my couch eating tortilla chips to living on the damn island.

God, rein it in, Etta. It's a second audition for a scholarship to a school you are not going to get into. You are not going to win a million dollars.

"I think Bianca's more upset about it than I am," Mason says. Under the table he traps my ankle between both of his. We're back at the retro coffee shop, drinking ice coffee because it's ridiculously warm for February today.

"She's just worried about you." I actually have no idea what she is. She was a little weepy and incoherent on the phone last night. I talked her down and we made plans to hang out after group tomorrow. But today I really just wanted to see Mason.

I don't know what we're doing. I think he's looking at this relationship or whatever more seriously than I am. Which is fine with me, but it does make me feel like I'm using him that I don't really feel the same way.

Watch, I'm actually a lesbian. That's the big punch line.

"I'm worried about her," he says. "Everything going on with James."

"What's going on with James?"

"Hooooo boy," he says.

"No no hey. What's going on with James?"

"He's hanging out with that guy a lot. Blue hair."

"Yeah?"

"Yeah. He lives just outside Bellevue and James has made the drive every day for the past three and he stays there for a few hours and like . . . you know. She's used to having him around all the time. And at first he'd bring her with him but then I think . . . I don't know. Either she stopped wanting to go or James stopped wanting her there."

I mean, I love Kristina, but I wouldn't want her hanging around on my dates. But I don't think that's what this is.

"She's having a rough time," Mason says. "The religious thing."

"Shit. Yeah."

"She needs to get over it," he says. "She will."

And I say, "Yeah," but I don't really know if it's that easy, or honestly that it should be. "You think she should?"

"I think . . ." He stops, actually thinks. "I think yeah, actually. James is more important to her than anything else, and if she lets this get between them she's gonna implode."

I don't know if you implode if there's nothing to you, first of all, but also, obviously thinking that gay people are wrong is antiquated and messed up, but that idea is not what Bianca's worshipping. She's not in this to hate gay people. She *doesn't* hate gay people. She's just this girl who really loves her God and doesn't want to do anything to pull herself away from him—sorry, Mason—probably just as much as she doesn't want to be pulled away from her brother. And yeah, we can ask her to deal with James being gay, we can ask her to *accept* it, but I don't think we can just say that something she believes, something that she fundamentally wants to not hurt anybody, is something she can, or should, just get over.

But you know, what do I know about God. My mom thinks that nothing's real if it's not in biology textbooks, and I guess I'm the same. But, to make a totally blasphemous analogy, I assume, knowing that there are ugly parts of Rachel doesn't make me love her any less, and it definitely doesn't make me want to do anything to screw up her chances of loving me.

But I mean, whatever. We do anyway.

"She'll be all right," I say, but I'm not really sure of that either.

Yeah, worries confirmed. Bianca's a wreck in group. I actually get her to sit down, which is kind of frightening in and of itself, but I think if I didn't she would have shaken until she fell over.

Now she's just sitting here next to me, tapping her feet and twisting around and jitterbugging her hands on her knees to burn more calories when she isn't pushing tissues into her eyes and breathing out hard through her mouth.

Angela's got her big authoritative group leader hat on and since Bianca hardly ever talks, everyone's really absorbed in this, halfway between concerned and fascinated, and Angela's trying to get Bianca to explain how she feels when all Bianca wants to do is put her head down and go to sleep.

"I just *miss* him," she says. "It's so *stupid*. And I'm just, I'm scared something's going to happen to him, or my parents are going to find out, or . . ."

"Have you talked to him about it?" Angela says.

Bianca shakes her head. "We don't talk about it." She's swallowing over and over. "I thought I was fine with it. I wanted to be fine with it."

"Have you told him you miss him?"

"I said we don't talk about it. H-he would say he was going to Bellevue to *visit that friend* and did I want to come with him so I came and we went to a restaurant a-and he was all, he was so nervous watching me like I was going to ruin it and was I going to eat and was I going to tell my parents and if we could just *talk* about it . . ."

I say, "Tell him you need him to do that for you."

"But . . ."

"But what, sweetheart?" Angela says.

"But after he says it we can't go back. I can't . . . I'm sorry, Etta."

"Shh, no."

Angela says, "What are you apologizing for?"

I say, "She's still working out if she thinks being gay is wrong. It's okay."

And then of course a bunch of the girls have to go and jump on her and wow, guys, this is *not* what she needs right now.

I say, "Hey. I'm the queer one here and I'm saying leave her alone. She's fucking fourteen. She doesn't hate anyone. She isn't running around telling people they're going to Hell. She's struggling because her damn *God* told her something she's questioning and that's really scary for her and she's *fourteen*. Leave her alone."

Leave her alone.

God, what am I doing.

There's this weight on my shoulder, then, this featherweight of her leaning into me, hiding in me.

"Shh shh shh," I say. "It's okay. We love you so much."

"I don't want to be like this," she says. "I want to be there for him."

"You are."

"He won't even talk to me, he . . . he chose him instead."

"It's not like that."

"I know it doesn't have to be," she says. "But he's acting like it does."

Angela's going on and on about how Bianca needs to be open about what she needs, but I'm getting the feeling Angela doesn't really understand what it means to grow up in a family that won't talk about anything real and how hard it is to get away from that, and I'm beginning to think Angela is maybe not the right person to counsel a group of girls who are starving themselves instead of trying to fix what's really wrong.

Something is really wrong with us.

I kiss Bianca's forehead and rub her back through the rest of the meeting.

She's better after group, when we're back in one of the practice rooms, her boom box, a piano, me. Our audition prep group has kind of fallen apart, now that Bee and James and me and this girl Lisa we don't really like are the only ones from our original group to get to second round. I guess we'll start meeting up and practicing again like we did, but I haven't seen James since the original audition—all I've seen is Bianca's phone pressed to her ear twice now, when she says *Jamie* and whisper-cries—so I'm wondering if Bianca maybe wasn't at least a little right about him disappearing.

But it doesn't seem right. He loves her so much.

It's just that I think Bianca's lost more weight, and I'm having a hard time not having issues with James about it.

There's a ballet barre in this room. "Show me something," Bianca says.

So I go to the barre and go through the different positions, and she tries to copy. This girl is not a good dancer. I laugh and go to her and hold her waist and say, "Here. Gently."

She's all floppy doll, like her bones are broken.

"Follow me," I say, and I stand in front of her on the barre and lead her through some stretches, pulling my toe up toward my head and bending into low pliés. I take my sneakers off and do some pas de bourrées across the floor and throw in some entrechats—basically these little jumps where you point your toes while you're in the air—because those are easy but look impressive. She sings parts of *The Nutcracker* under her breath, the "Dance of the Sugar Plum Fairy" that everyone knows, and I turn pirouettes because everyone knows pirouettes.

"You've got to start dancing again, Etta."

I flop down onto the floor. "That was more ballet than I've done in ages."

"And you're happy, look at you."

"Just tired," I say, but I am. I'm lying on my back so happy because of a few pirouettes. How did I ever get through ballet classes without smiling my damn face off from the fact that I was *here, dancing, good at something*? Right, I was too busy being self-conscious for being the biggest girl there, but it's not like I was overexaggerating five pounds or something, you know? I was significantly bigger than the other girls, and I definitely would be now.

"Girls who look like me don't do ballet," I say.

She shrugs and tucks her legs underneath her. "Girls who look like me do, but that doesn't mean I can, y'know?"

"Conclusion: neither of us can do ballet."

"If this were a test I would give you an F minus."

I get up and do more stretches in front of the mirror, focusing on the way my leg muscles hold taut. "I do miss it," I say. "It scares me how much."

"Because you're afraid you don't remember how?"

I shake my head. "I'm afraid that I might be really happy."

"Why is that so scary?" she says, not like she's judging me, but like this is driving her crazy, like she just doesn't understand why we can't let ourselves have everything and Bianca, honey, come on.

"Because that means we *exist*."

I'm pouring my measured glass of whole milk with breakfast when my mom startles me with this sharp little "Etta" that makes me jump and spill my milk everywhere and awesome, Mom, thank you, this is my only uniform shirt that fits me right now. I'm going to smell like old cheese all day. Whatever. They already hate me.

I mop myself up in front of the sink and she says, "When were you going to tell me about this audition?"

"Oh. Ha! I honestly kind of thought I had."

"You *kind of thought you had*?"

"I'm trying to be honest, okay? I wasn't, like, intentionally hiding this from you. I figured you knew for some reason and it never came up."

Kristina looks up from her eggs. "Auditioning for what?"

"Brentwood."

"You got an audition?"

"It's a different process," I say. "Cattle call. Moooo." Get it, 'cause I'm chubby and covered in milk. Now I can't stop laughing to myself a little—seriously, the covered in milk part—and I can tell by Mom's face that she will be having none of my levity right now, thanks.

"What's a cattle call?" Kristina says.

"It just means like open audition. You could have tried out! We're on second round now."

"Boarding school with theater kids? My spot would probably be better used for someone who wouldn't want to run for the hills after twenty-four hours."

"Aw, but then who's gonna visit me once I get in?" I feel my mom staring at me, so I say, "I'm not going to get in, will you relax? I'm sure there's like thousands of people auditioning."

"I still wish you'd asked me before—"

"You let me apply every year and never put on this kind of . . . performance about it."

"Etta, you know why it's different now."

"I . . . have completely no idea why it's different now."

She waves her hand at me, at my refilled glass of milk, at my . . . what?

"What are you talking about?"

She says, "Are you sure that you're really . . . healthy enough to leave home?"

You're kidding me.

You've got to be freaking kidding me.

For three years I starved myself and she never noticed and she took those calls from the worried school counselor and told him I was fine, just *fine, you know how teenagers go through these phases, probably for attention, I'll talk to her about her body image,* like a five-minute talk about *loving yourself for who you are and choosing food that makes you feel good!* was going to fix me, for three years we did that shit—no, I did that shit without her, and now that I have stepped up and I'm getting help on my own—and yeah, so what if I'm a little self-righteous about it, this is a big deal and I get to act like it is—*now* I'm too screwed-up to go away?

I repeat that in my head over and over until all the air's let out of it, until I don't need to say it anymore. I just say something else, something that's also true, something that's not going to hurt her.

"I mean it," I say. "I'm not going to get in. I'm just doing it with some friends."

And then she smiles, this real little smile, and says, "You made new friends?"

So I tell her all about them—watered-down, beefed-up—and I watch her keep smiling and nodding and approving and I pretend it's for me.

I'm washing my hands in the second-floor bathroom that morning when I hear something click, that screechy noise of a chair being pushed around on the floor. Giggling.

I try to push the door open to see what the hell is going on, but it won't budge.

They locked me in here.

I'm going to be late for calculus. I'm going to be late for the only good part of my school day, and what's infuriating the hell out of me is that I can't see who's out there, and I can't see who is doing this to me, I don't even know if it's the Dykes, and any hope of it being some random prank is dashed by muffled voices I can't recognize going *what are you gonna do now, Etta?* and God, what are they gaining from this?

Rachel Rachel Rachel come on, come stop them—

But she doesn't, because classes have started and the voices have stopped, it's just me and this door and whatever the hell they shoved against it to keep it from opening, godDAMN it, how is it that I don't weigh enough to get this door open.

It hurts my shoulder. "God*damn* it!"

I'm about to text my little sister, my baby damn sister who shouldn't be at all involved in this, and then I hear some teacher, either Mrs. Mackey or Mrs. Patrone—they're

practically identical even when you're looking right at them —
say, "Hello? Is there anyone in there? Is someone locked in
there?"

I close my eyes. "Yeah." My voice cracks.

The chair screeches away and the door swings open. "Etta.
Everything all right?"

"Uh-huh."

"Etta."

"We were just playing a game. I have to go."

I don't go to calculus. I go to the parking lot and curl up in
my backseat and later I get written up for skipping.

14

THERE'S A LECTURE AT SCHOOL AND THEY TALK ABOUT THESE
zero-tolerance-for-bullying things and for a few days no one
really bothers me, and I don't think I noticed how much it
actually was bothering me, on this quiet, everyday kind of level,
until it stopped. Now the other girls at school seem to have lost
interest (if only the boys texting me asking me out would do
the same, whatever) and when I walk into the room the Dykes
just roll their eyes and whisper to each other with all this fake
animation because yeah, it's really so exciting to see me the
fourth time today, come on, you don't have anything new to say
about me because you've been saying the same shit for like four
months now and I haven't given you any new material. Rachel
comes to school sporadically. She's going to get in trouble if she
keeps that up, and it's hard to not feel guilty about that.

I keep to myself, hold my head down, get good grades, sneak into the music room and practice singing "At the Ballet" during my study periods. It's fine.

But I guess the Dykes get bored of being relatively civil the same way the other girls got bored of me (and why does that bother me, that I don't get that attention anymore, Jesus, I am seriously deranged—that thing I said to James about there being something wrong with me?) because about a week after the first audition Natasha corners me at my locker and says, "We had a question for you."

Except the rest of them aren't around, which somehow makes this actually kind of scary. There's something about Tasha—she's tall, dark hair, not naturally pretty but knows how to do her makeup well enough that people think she is— that's always been kind of terrifying. Maybe it was that I always knew she wanted to be where I was.

But right now, maybe it's that I'm all out of the way, Natasha, okay, I'm not even bothering you at all, so why are you breaking this ugly little truce we've had *now*?

"We heard you're trying out for Brentwood," she says.

Wow, Natasha, what lovely detective work, I try out *every year*. She doesn't need to know this year is different. It's not like she's studied their audition process. Or maybe she has. God, that would be weird and not totally out of character. Natasha's so creepy. How did we even *find* her? (She was listening to the Indigo Girls on her iPod so loudly we could hear it a few lockers away in our first week of freshman year, that's how. Natasha puts the "Dyke" in Dyke).

"Yeah, because you're so concerned with what I do."

"We just saw you on the bus and then did a little investigating," she says, with this voice like "investigating" is the most disgusting thing she could say, when it's about me. You'd think she was saying "blow jobs" by the way she says each syllable like she can't stand to have it in her mouth any longer.

"Well, mission accomplished, then." I root around my locker for my books. It still smells like dead chickens in here.

"So we have that figured out," she says. "Now we're just wondering about that girl you were with."

I close the door and spin my lock. "What girl?"

"Come on, you fucking know what girl."

"Why do you care?"

"Are you fucking her?"

"Like I would tell you if I was."

"It would be in your best interests to."

"Oh yeah? And why's that?"

"Because," she says. "Because Rachel's the one who wanted to know."

I stick my tongue into my cheek. "So you're Rachel's little errand girl, huh? *Ouch.*"

It happens before I have time to react, because I wasn't expecting it, Natasha's arm coming down hard on my collarbone and slamming me back into the lockers. She holds me there, forearm right under my neck, her nails digging into my shoulder.

Ouch.

"That's better than what you are," Natasha says. "She doesn't even love you anymore."

"That's not true," I say, before I realize that I should have said *I don't care.*

Natasha rolls her eyes and lets me go. "She probably just wanted you to find some new girl so she could stop worrying that you'd die alone. Not like you can keep a boy, right?"

"How's that virginity treating you, Tasha?" It's a low blow, and it's not like I actually think being a virgin is a problem. I just think being Tasha is a problem, and her virginity happens to be topical.

Plus it never, ever fails to rile her up. "Bite me," she says.

"You'd love if I did."

She spits in my hair—stay classy, Tasha—and saunters away. Yeah, whatever, because it's hard to get that nonchalant thing back when everyone here just saw you shove the pariah into a locker.

I rub my collarbone a little and check my watch. It's one thirty. Rachel has study period next, and she always spends the first five minutes of it in the third-floor bathroom brushing her hair and doing her insulin shot. I don't even know for sure if she's here today, though.

Can't hurt to check.

• • •

"Did you send Natasha to interrogate me?"

Rachel barely looks up. She pushes the plunger down on the needle, pulls the needle out, rubs the spot on her stomach. When I was ten I learned how to give her shots just in case, but I've never had to. For some reason I'm right now obsessed with the idea that maybe Natasha has at some point. I'm so *weird*.

"I didn't send her to interrogate you," she says eventually. "I sent her because I was worried about you."

"You don't have to be worried about me. I'm fine. I got a second audition."

She looks away from the mirror, where she was examining her teeth. "That's great, Etta."

She still does it to me. "Thanks."

"Did that girl you were with get one too?"

Here we go. "Her name's Bianca. And yeah."

"Are you guys . . ."

"Why do you care, Ray?"

And why don't I just say *no*? Is it because I wish that I were? Is it because I think on some level we *are*?

No, I think it's because if Rachel knew I wasn't, she wouldn't have any interest in talking to me. I think it's because standing in a bathroom arguing with her is the closest I've felt to her in months.

"She looked . . . young."

"Yeah, she is."

"And she looked sick."

"Sick" is coded here. I'm not an idiot.

Rachel says, "Listen, obviously it's your life or whatever and you know what you're doing, and if she makes you happy, that's all that matters."

Pause to consider the fact that me dating a fourteen-year-old anorexic is okay but me dating a guy is not.

Rachel. What are you even *doing*? You can't really care this much about this shit. You just can't. I don't think the Dykes are even thinking about it anymore as much as they're just following through with what they started. Isabel insulting my shoes is not really topical to me sleeping with a guy.

"You've just been doing really well, and I just want you to think about if this is healthy for you," Rachel says, and like, how the hell would she know if I'm doing well? Is she just judging by the fact that I haven't lost any weight? But I can't be too mad about it because the truth is, yeah, I am doing really well. It's screwed up and horrible sometimes and some days it's a million times harder than just starving would be but I'm doing it, and the most ridiculous part of this entire intervention is that one of the biggest reasons I'm being so good about recovery is for Bianca. I mean, Jesus, *fourteen*. She needs a good influence. And I've already messed up pretty bad with Kristina—*hey, little sis, cover for me while I puke in our childhood bathroom*—so yeah, maybe this is my second chance.

Rachel climbs up onto the sinks and sits there. We're ten

years old again, all of a sudden. "I don't want you slipping again," she says. "I think it's important that you keep your eye on what's important, you know? But if she makes you happy, that's really good, Etta. You should be with a girl who makes you happy."

You should be with a girl *who makes you happy.*

"We're not ten," I say.

"What?"

"You and me. We're not ten. *I'm* not ten. I could fall back in love with Sherrie whatever her last name was—"

"Sher."

"Her name was not Sherrie Sher."

"It really was."

"Well all right, being Mrs. Sherrie Sher wouldn't bring me back to who I was. I could date all the girls in the world and it's still not going to change the fact that when you look at me you see a guy on top of me."

It's still about that to Rachel.

I know her.

She really cares about this shit.

"Etta . . ."

"So why are we even pretending like this redemption thing is possible? You guys dumped me. I'm dealing with it. Are you?"

I don't know what I was expecting, but it was not for Rachel to be off the counter, to be on the floor with me, to have her hands in my hair and her forehead bent down to mine—what is with these girls with their hands on me today? Except this is so not Natasha. This is so, so different from Natasha.

She kisses me, for a long time. It's not a deep kiss, not a sexy kiss. That would be a lot easier.

"Shut up," she says. "Okay? Just shut up."

I do, for a while, just listen to her breathing and feel her touching me.

Eventually I say, "I'm taking care of her. Bianca. And she's getting better. She's in group with me."

Rachel nods. My face moves with hers. "That's good. That's really good."

"*She's* good." I don't know why I say this next part. "You'd really like her."

The thing is, I think that she would.

The thing is that Rachel has good taste and her kissing me makes me feel beautiful again.

And it would be one of the last things she'd ever want to inspire, but feeling like that is enough to make me go home after school and dig my toe shoes out of the backyard.

15

I PUT MY SHOES ON AND PRACTICE JUST STANDING UP, FLEXING my ankles around, taking small steps around the room. I'm in my carpeted bedroom, so it's pretty stupid, but at least this gives me an excuse to do a shitty job, which I kind of do.

I feel so stupid about doing this. The goal right now should be to ace this next audition, and there's absolutely no way ballet is going to help me there. The dancing, if there even is any at this stage—Bianca says last time she got to second round, it was just singing—is just going to be another step combination. The next time I'd really use ballet would be if I got into the school—a school that, I've always known, has a pretty mediocre dance program—and if I can't sing, I can't get into the school. I should really be applying to dance schools.

Oh.

I should be applying to dance schools.

I've been putting it off because I really don't think I could take being surrounded by ballerinas all the time. Even when I was pre-professional, I kind of hated it. I don't think I can look at them and know how much prettier they are than me and how much an audience would rather watch them move around, these tall lean girls that form straight lines and swoop through the air, than watch all however-many-pounds-of-me jiggle her way through tours chaînés déboulés. You're not supposed to look at a girl's body when she dances, not in that way. She's supposed to be unobtrusive. She's supposed to just be part of the music, and here I come in all attention-grabbing and ETTAETTAETTA and you can make that sound as awesome and special-snowflakey as you want but at the end of the day that's not what people want ballerinas to be. Rachel knew that, saw that pressure getting to me. That's why I quit.

Except I keep dancing and then I go over to my computer and look up ballet schools in New York City (I haven't done this in years, seriously, but it takes me right back to being that little twelve-year-old drinking her strawberry milk and staring at these same damn web pages, flexing her feet under the desk) and I think, okay, I'm going to table that. That's a thing. Waiting until college to get out, after these past few weeks, is beginning to seem almost as nonviable as staying here indefinitely.

I turn on "At the Ballet" as I close the tabs about schools, a nice segue between fantasy (ballet) and reality (practicing for the audition—yeah, yeah, yeah, I know, how is that less fantasy, shut up). Mom and Kristina are home, so I stuff pillows under the door so they won't hear me because I don't want their comments right now about how I "sounded really nice today!" because I can never tell whether or not they're telling the truth or if they just feel sorry for me, and I sing through Sheila's part like always but then I'm too busy twirling around on the floor again to go back to the beginning of the song like I usually do, and for the first time I hear the entire thing.

I don't remember the name of the girl who sings second. She doesn't say it, and I think Bianca mentioned it at some point but I only hung on to Sheila because Bianca said she was the important one. "She's the personality of the song," Bianca said. "She has this whole monologue before it starts where she hits on the director and everything. She's awesome and untouchable and damaged. You can totally act her."

The second girl is nice, and then there's someone else singing with her, harmonizing through a bit about everyone being beautiful at the ballet. Which is a nice sentiment and everything, except, you know, the ballet was where I wasn't pretty at all.

But when I was a kid, spinning around in my room like I am now, ballet was my entire, beautiful world.

And then all of a sudden someone's speaking. She's talking about when she was a little kid, and she had this shitty broken home but she got through it by dancing around her living room with her arms held like she had someone to dance with, even when she didn't. She's got this New York accent and this small, honest little voice, and she doesn't sound bitter or sarcastic about her fantastic fantasy life. She's just this girl who's feeling all this shit and who still gets this big kick out of holding her arms out and was never ashamed about doing it.

There's some harmonies here, some doo doo doos, and I dance around like I'm waltzing instead of like I'm a ballerina because I'm ridiculous.

And then all of a sudden she's singing, all by herself. Maggie, she says.

> *Everything was beautiful at the ballet*
> *Raise your arms, and someone's always there*

She doesn't slide up to a higher note at the end of the refrain like I was expecting, like the other two girls did.

> *At the ballet*

That one hits harder, higher.

> *At the ballet!*

Jesus. It's a really, really, *really* high note, and she's singing it strong and solid, like a yell, like she does not give a shit about being pretty, she just has to shoot this note out right now because she is singing about the ballet and it is wringing her out.

I try the high note, but I can't do it, not unless I do it breathy and muted and not at all how it's supposed to be. I can't do it. Which is fine, because this singing part is shorter than Sheila's and not nearly as easy to act through.

But it's not Sheila's part that I listen to over and over again as I lie flat on my bed, pointing and repointing my feet in my shoes, listening to Maggie through my headphones shouting about the ballet. Maggie. I love you, you imaginary little fantasy girl.

I call Bianca later to tell her about digging my shoes up and about how long it took me to listen to the whole song and is there any way she thinks I could maybe learn to hit that note before the audition next week and oh who am I kidding, I've already practiced Sheila a hundred times and this is the plan, but Bianca doesn't pick up her cell phone. I call her house instead, and this scary-proper man tells me that Bianca isn't available right now, but would I like to talk to James?

"Hey," James says.

"Hey. Where's Bee?"

"She's here, Dad's just not letting her use the phone because apparently she disrespected him or something, I don't know."

"*Bianca* did?"

"She went to church without us this morning because she's the only one who isn't okay with skipping ever, and she came home crying or something about how she thinks God hates her because she isn't Bianca-ish enough or something? And Dad took it as some kind of personal affront that Bianca would say that God hates her so of course the answer to that is to yell at her. Freudian parallels much, Dad?"

"Ouch. What happened at church?"

"I don't know, I wasn't there. I told my parents I was sick and went to Bellevue."

There's a lot of things I want to say to that but none that aren't bitchy and so out of line or so completely not *fair*, because, like, how dare you have a boyfriend, James! How dare you care about something besides Bianca? I mean, come on. The last thing Bianca needs is us making her into the kind of delicate little heroine we need to drop our lives to protect. The problem is that I don't like to think about what might happen to her if we *don't*, and maybe that's a lot more important than making sure she's not too codependent. I'll take codependent over starving herself until she's locked in some institution, or worse, y'know?

I'm just saying that all of that: the moral of the story is that we can't babysit Bianca! stuff would be nice and all, but I'm not willing to sacrifice my friend to it. If she needs this, I'll be this.

I have a little sister. This isn't new.

(This is a reason not to fall apart.)

And James should be okay with this too, and I'm sorry if that's unfair, except that I'm kind of not.

So I just say, "How come Ian never comes here?"

"Because here is such an exciting place!"

"Like Bellevue is."

"You have a point."

"Seriously, though, Bee misses having you around and I do too. And I know Mason does. He calls me all like 'let's talk about Mrs. Hampdon being a bitch' and I am like 'Mason I do not go to your school.'"

He laughs. "She isn't even a bitch, she's very nice, actually. Mason just never shows up and then is all indignant when she fails him."

"Damn educators."

"Seriously."

I say, "She's not doing well, is she?"

"Yeah. I don't . . . It's not like she ever was, y'know? She's not you."

"I think for a while I thought everyone in my group was there to get better."

"Yeah, most people are forced into it. She used to pout in the car the whole way home after."

She doesn't try.

Why did I think that I would be the thing to save her? All I can do is watch.

But it's better than her going down alone, you know? If I can't pull her up, and if I refuse to get pulled down with her, the least I can do is hold her hand.

"I want to meet Ian," I say. "I only even know his name because I've been creepy and weird about it."

"He wants to meet you too! I talk about you."

"You do?"

"Hey, you're my friend."

"Bring him to a prep session sometime or something. Bianca and I have been practicing our asses off. She makes me sing until my throat's sore."

"Your throat wouldn't be sore if your technique was better."

"Ew, you sound just like her."

"How about I bring him to a non-prep session? There's an Irish pub by our school. You know it?"

Like there's anywhere I don't know in this town. "Yeah, I know it." It's pretty close to Cupcake. I should take everyone to Cupcake after. I am *so not being serious*, I do not want them to catch airborne STDs.

"There, tomorrow night? You want to tell Mason or should I?"

"Is this your way of asking about our relationship?"

"So there is a relationship."

"I don't know." I pull off my shoes and find some nail polish. If we're going to gossip about boys, I'm going to paint my toenails, thanks. "I don't think so."

"Do you want there to be?"

"Nope. I'm happy, he's happy, we're having fun. Why, has he been hinting around at something?"

"I don't know, I don't think so. He's generally fine with casual."

"See, I am too. Everyone wins."

He pauses. "It seems like you should want more."

"Do you have any idea how gay you sound right now? You meet the right guy and immediately want to get married. Are you sure you're not a lesbian?"

"Hey, you'd know better than I would. Expert."

"What does a lesbian bring on the second date?"

"Uh, what?"

"A moving van."

He laughs. "I wouldn't even need a moving van. Back of the pickup truck: mattress, piano, Bianca, good to go."

"This is honestly the gayest conversation of my life."

"Making you homesick?"

"A little bit!"

"Call Rachel."

"Ughhh."

"Aren't you guys getting somewhere? Call her."

"I don't know. Maybe I shouldn't push it."

"Do you, um. Have a thing for her?"

I sigh. "It's complicated."

"That means yes."

"No, it doesn't, it means it's complicated." What am I even supposed to say? I don't have a thing for her unless "having a thing for her" means "having a life that revolves around her" way more than it means anything sexual. If I picture a happy relationship with anyone, the thing is . . . the thing is, it's Danielle, this girl-turned-memory who's sitting in New York drinking espresso or reading her psychology textbook or whatever she's doing up there. It was simple with her. Until it wasn't. It's different with Rachel. It always has been.

The irony of the entire situation is that I think if Danielle were still in Nebraska I wouldn't be running quite as fast, at least. Or maybe we would have broken up even without the move. Seventeen-year-olds don't tend to stay together until death do us part, no matter what our sweet baby James here seems to think.

"Maybe you should invite her out with us," James says.

"I'm really incredibly not going to do that. Mason, remember?"

"I thought you weren't a thing."

I am not going to say that Rachel is only talking to me because she thinks I'm dating James's sister. Nope.

So I just say, "Do your parents know about you and Ian?" even though I know the answer.

"Oh God no. Oh *God* no."

"Be caaareful."

"Yeah, I'm in my room, door locked, et cetera."

"Bianca's not going to tell them?"

"Of course not. Bianca's Team Me Against the World. Always has been."

"Always will be."

"Yeah."

The thing is that we have no idea what "always" is going to end up meaning for Bianca. Maybe I'm just now starting to get that this girl is really sick.

Like, physically, bone-deep sick.

"Tomorrow night," I say.

"Yeah, you got it, kid."

It's becoming clearer and clearer at school that something's going on with Kristina. I think maybe there's some ramifications of whatever went down with that boy, and a lot of the stuff I'm seeing from her friends is pretty disgustingly similar to stuff that's been happening with me this year. Do not taunt my sister when she's getting her books, you assholes, I will end you.

Except before I get over to her, Rachel's there, all of a sudden, putting all of her sixty-eight inches between Kristina and the freshmen, talking their shit down. And they finally back off and Rachel turns to Kristina and wraps her in this hug.

16

IAN, JAMES, AND BIANCA ARE ALREADY AT THE PUB WHEN I GET
there, and Mason shows up a while after. (I'm the one who
told him, but I was coming from chorus so we didn't come
together. It doesn't mean anything.) We pull an extra chair up
to this little circular table and I have my fake ID ready but the
waitress clearly doesn't care and brings a pitcher of beer to the
table, whaaat why do I never come to this place? It helps that
Mason looks pretty old. Mmm, he looks good tonight.

There's a piano in the corner and after two glasses of beer
James shows us why he needed to bring his piano in his fantasy
moving van and damn, he is good. Bianca leans her head against
my shoulder and we listen while he bangs out songs and sings
and the other people in the pub are at least good-natured about
it and I say to her, "How come you don't play piano, huh?"

"I took violin for a little but I hated it. Mom let me stop."

"Ugh, my mom never let me quit anything."

"You quit ballet."

"Yeah, when I was too old for her to stop me. And she never had to talk me into that in the first place. Plus, I dug my shoes up, so who knows. Potentially un-quitting."

Bianca sits up. "You did?"

Ian says, "Wait, were they actually buried?"

"Yeah, in my backyard."

"Aren't they all full of worms or whatever?"

"No! My best friend and I buried them and we made a coffin and everything. Wrapped duct tape around a shoe box, buried it, made a little gravestone. 'Here lies Etta's subjugation to the masculine ideals of beauty.'"

Mason says, "You guys blame us for everything."

Ian says, "That's what ballet's about?"

"I'm beginning to think maybe not," I say.

James comes back to the table and kisses the top of my head, then Bianca's, then Ian's, then, after a shrug, Mason's. Mason laughs and tackles him back into his seat. "Mason plays piano," James says while Mason's sitting on him to pin him down.

"You do?"

"Uh-huh, he's really good. Play us a yarn, Mason."

Mason rolls his eyes and heads over to the piano, and I don't know what he's singing (it's not show-tuney, huh) but it's nice, especially with all the beer. I rest my head on James's shoulder.

"So you two," Ian says, gesturing between James and me, "must be soul mates of some kind?"

"Whaaat?" I kiss James's arm. "No such thing."

"Etta is our fairy godmother," James says.

I say, "Etta's making this group *slightly* less white."

"Nah, come on, you know why I say that," Ian says.

I say, "No, we really do not."

"Come on! Etta James!"

"Ha!" James says, and then he and I burst into "At Last" together, obviously. Bianca joins in, sinking into the low notes, and Mason's immediately playing it on the piano, and I see Bianca smile at Ian and then James, and maybe it's not as good as smiling at Ian and James *together*, but this girl is trying so hard. And I can tell she really does like Ian, and that this would be a different issue if she didn't. But she does, and she wants to like them together, and maybe that's all that this takes. I look at Mason. Maybe we really don't have to think this much. After all, Bianca obviously hasn't touched the beer (not that we'd let her, eating disorder aside, come on! Fourteen!) and she still looks loose, happy.

"Brave girl," I say into her hair, and she smiles.

"So!" Ian says. "Audition! What are we doing?"

"'At the Ballet.'"

"Sheila?"

"Yep. I've got the disenchanted overqualified dancer thing down. Maybe I can convince them it's true!"

James says, "You are totally overqualified where dancing's concerned."

"But I am *not* disenchanted."

Bianca says, "'Let's Hear It For the Boy.' Like always."

"I'm out," Mason says. "But it's all right."

"Okay, but I knew all of those already, I'm bored," I say. "What about you two?"

James groans. "I don't knooow."

"He does something different every time," Bianca says. "It's dumb."

"You're not afraid they'll get sick of you?" James says. "Like, every year this girl shows up and sings 'Let's Hear It for the Boy.'"

"No. I know I'm good at it."

James says, "Yeah, I guess it did get you in."

I say, "What?"

"I didn't tell her that," Bianca says, narrowing her eyes at him.

He says, "Sorry, sorry," but obviously doesn't think it's a big deal.

She rips at her napkin a little. "Yeah, well. I got in last year."

"Did you go to New York?" I say, like that's the important part, God, Etta.

She shakes her head. "Chicago for the final audition and then I got in."

"Why didn't you go?"

"That wasn't a scholarship."

Oh.

"She was too sick, anyway," James says, tucking her head against his shoulder. "We might not have even let her."

She just shrugs.

God.

"That's so shitty," I say. "That sucks."

"You'll get in this year, Bee," Mason says. James nods, and I think, *she was sicker than this last year. She has been sicker than this.*

Or at least that's what they're telling themselves.

"I just wish it were in Nebraska," Bianca says.

I don't get that. I just don't get that so much. I'm going for this audition full speed ahead now, I guess, but I still feel pretty crappy sitting here and knowing that what these guys want so much is to be singers and to go to that school and soak it all up and what I want is just to be in New York. Like, come on, Etta, this is their dream and you're using it as your Get-out-of-Nebraska-free card. I guess I can at least take solace in the fact that there is no way I'm going to get in over them. No harm, no foul, right?

"So what are you going to sing?" I ask James.

"Right now I'm leaning toward 'Santa Fe.' You and Mason inspired me."

Mason and I start singing it again and I say, "Ooooh. Can you do the octave jump at the beginning?" to James.

"What? Of course."

"I saw *someone on Broadway* who couldn't do the octave jump." The first time Collins sings the chorus, he's supposed to do it an octave down, and then immediately he's *whoosh* up into the octave where he stays for the rest of the song. It sounds *so* cool and I don't know why anyone gets away with not doing it. Probably because it's really damn hard.

"Sing for us, James!" I say, and he laughs and sings the first part of it, all soft, but hell if he doesn't get that octave. We cheer and pound on the table and I think the people around us aren't as tolerant anymore, so good thing he sang quietly!

"What about you?" Bianca asks Ian. You go, Bianca.

He says, "I'm thinking 'Springtime for Hitler.' How bizarre is that?

"From *The Producers?*" Mason says.

"Yep."

"The song about it being . . ."

"Springtime for Hitler. Yep. I'm hoping the judges have a sense of humor. I can't sing as well as most of the people auditioning. I have to get by on novelty."

"Like me!" I say.

James rolls his eyes. "You're both good."

I say, "Yeah, and if 'good' were enough we'd all be in no question."

Mason, back at the table with us now, fake-pouts, and I kick him.

"You're lovely," I whisper to him, and then I kiss him, just because I can, just because it feels right.

He kisses me back, a little too long, and then says, "You want to get out of here?"

It's a more complicated question than I would have expected, because being here has been this amazing thing I haven't had since the heyday of me and the Dykes, back when we just had *fun* together. We'd sit around Titania's house on her big rug and do our nails and giggle or we'd go to Cupcake and dance in slutty circles or we'd sit on Rachel's roof and look up at the stars. Maybe it's just the recent stuff poisoning my memories of them, but really I'm not sure it was ever quite as perfect as this. Because the only thing that made me the same as any of them besides Rachel was that we all liked to sleep with girls, and then here I am with a bunch of people who I actually have more than one thing in common with, who are actually interested in the same things as me (musical theater! Being queer! Not eating!) and what do I care really if they're all doing them better? They still like me. We're auditioning for the same however-many-spaces but we're not competitive. We're just being together. We're just being happy that the other ones exist.

So that's amazing, but at the same time there's this boy smiling at me and everything makes sense, just for this min-ute, and I make a choice not to overthink it. Be an example to Bianca, get myself some action, but I really don't think it's because I want to show this stupid damn boy that I can think less. I think I really just am doing this for me.

"Yeah," I say. "I want to get out of here."

He's good at sex. I've slept with a decent handful of people—only him and Ben for guys, though—and had a great time with a bunch of them but I'm not sure any of them have been as objectively good at sex as Mason is. Maybe Rachel, after a while, but all we knew was stuff the other one taught us, so there was a weird sense of déjà vu and self-consciousness about it all the time, like, does that feel as good to her when I do it? Why is she doing that thing with her tongue that only feels kind of okay? Wait, do *I* do that thing with my tongue that only feels kind of okay?

But Mason. Mason is good. He cradles me, in this way I've never felt and never thought that I'd like, and he pushes boundaries without asking but in a *good* way, in this patient way, this slow way, but I fall into it, I let him explore, I just *trust* him. I don't love him, but there is something about being with him that just works, that is just so *right now*, and the truth is that I am kind of in love with right now. I am just so goddamn happy with where my life is, and I am so happy with where I am, and being here in this bed with this boy and feeling high and low and beautiful . . . It is just not hard to love where I am when where I am is here.

After, he kisses my neck and holds me, my head tucked under his chin. He twists my dreads between his fingers.

"Feels nice," I say.

"So does this. You on me."

"Mmm-hmm." I snuggle closer, push my face into his chest. I don't feel fat. It helps that he isn't so skinny either, now that he's undressed, and he's just okay with it, and that he held on to every bit of me like he would miss it if it weren't there, like sex with me wouldn't work as well if there were not as much of me.

I just like this.

"I like your house," he says, which is funny because all he's seen is this room. We climbed up through the window because my mom is asleep (she goes to bed at like ten) and we didn't want to deal with sneaking in the front door with Kristina around. It was easy but added to the whole feeling that we're doing something secret and wrong when whatever, as if my mom would really care all that much. Better him than a girl!

"It's too big," I say. "For three of us."

"Just you and your mom and your sister?" he says, with that *where's your dad* so implied.

"He left when I was really little," I say. "It's fine. He lives a few blocks over but I never see him. It's pretty stupid."

"My dad died when I was nine," he says.

"Shit, I'm sorry."

"Thanks. It's okay. Our house is too big too. And he had all this money put away that I don't think my mom even knew about until he died, and if that's not sketchy as hell I don't know what is—"

"Ha. Yeah."

"But now it's all really, like, gratuitous."

I have a feeling I know why he's talking about this.

"I had no idea she got in," I say.

"I didn't either."

"Seriously?"

"No. They never told me."

"It's messed up. That she didn't get to go."

"Yeah." He stretches his legs a little, kicks his knees into my feet. "I get why they didn't tell me, you know?"

"Yeah. Me too."

"There's a part of this we're never going to understand. I mean, poor us, but still. I do feel like shit about it sometimes. Have you seen their house?"

"Uh-uh."

"I mean it's . . . you know. Fine."

"Yeah."

"It's not something I ever think about," he says. "And I think maybe that's kind of awful of me."

"How come you go to public school?" I say.

He laughs. "It's not a bad school."

"I'm trained to think that public schools are evil decrepit

places where people will stab you if you don't buy their drugs."

"Oh, well then yeah, if you think *that* counts as bad."

I kick back.

"I guess you're used to being surrounded by rich people," he says. "At your school."

"I think it's the black thing, honestly. If you're not *in* your prep school uniform, like wearing it at that exact moment, no one would guess that you could afford it. Can I tell you something?"

"Course."

"I get kind of pissed about it with James sometimes, or with the Dykes, even, to this extent, because . . . I mean, James goes on these *it's so hard to be gay* monologues, and like, obviously I get it, it's hard, but at the end of the day he can walk into a store and act straight and he's a white male again who's going to get treated like a white male, and there is nothing I can do to walk into a store and not be a black girl."

"Okay, but like, at least then everything's out in the open. You don't have to do that moment when you slip up and say something and see 'shit, I didn't know you were black' across their faces."

"Yeah, but—"

"And like your family is black, right? Your mom's family?"

"What's your point?"

"Easy, all right?"

I'm not a freaking horse, but I nod. And try not to breathe like one.

He says, "It's not like James has a whole family of gay people. He's got this thing that makes him different from all these people who are close to him."

"'This thing.' You make it sound like some disease."

"Oh, come on. So now you're indignant bisexual at me? You really can't play this from both sides."

"Yeah, I can. I have to. This is my damn life."

He gives me this sympathetic pout and yeah, okay, rein it in, Ett. This is not debate team. (I was strongly discouraged from joining debate team in middle school because they guessed— correctly—that I was too scary for other twelve-year-olds.)

So I say, "But you're right. The money thing."

"I don't know. It's hard to look around every day and be like *gee, I'm so thankful!* It doesn't mean we forget we're lucky, it just means we're not annoying about it."

"Yeah, except I bet Bianca and James think we're annoying for not doing that."

"Bianca and James don't give a shit what anyone else does," he says. "Bianca and James are Bianca and James. All they care about is each other."

"Sounding a little bitter, there."

"Yeah, well, you're friends with them. You know."

"What about Ian, though?"

"I don't know." He rolls over onto his side, brings me with him. "Could be a game changer. As could Brentwood, obviously."

"This is kind of their only chance, right?"

"There's always scholarships you can apply for. And maybe they'll do a cattle call again next year."

"Yeah. Maybe."

"What, you gonna drop out to give them a better shot?"

"Maybe."

"If you can convince the other hundreds of people who got through to do the same, then you've got a real plan going!"

"Yeah, shut it."

"You can't base your decisions on them. Then you're no better than they are."

"Who says I want to be?"

He kisses my forehead and looks at me. "You have to be," he says. "They're great, but we both know they're going down together."

"Maybe not anymore," I say.

"Yeah," Mason says. "Yeah, he could be a game changer."

Later I'm sneaking him out the window and I turn around and there's Kristina leaning against my door in her robe, managing to yawn and look judgmental at the same time.

"I'm dating him," I say. "Kind of."

"Did I say anything?"

"Stood there looking at me like I'm a slut."

"Etta, if you're going to make such a big deal out of not being ashamed that you're a slut, you should probably stop getting mad when people think you're a slut."

Huh. "Get out of here with your logic, it's past your bedtime."

"I'm fifteen, not five, and I *was* asleep."

"Scoot."

"*Someone* woke me up with all that 'uhhh uhhh oh my God yeeees.'"

"That mother of ours. What a hussy."

Kristina laughs. "Sleep well, Ett."

"You too."

I go to bed happy.

17

BIANCA CALLS ME BETWEEN FIFTH AND SIXTH PERIOD. "CAN YOU come get me?" She's crying. Hard.

"Bee. Are you sick? Where are you?"

"School. Come get me?"

"Where's James?"

"My parents came and got him."

That really does not sound good.

"Please, Etta."

It's a good thing I'm (half-seriously) planning to run away to New York in the next few months no matter what happens because there is no way I'm going to get into college with all this school I'm skipping.

"Of course, baby. I'm coming."

"No phones during school hours, *Etta*," Natasha says,

and she shoves me into the stone wall so hard I feel dizzy, and then she grabs me by the back of the shirt and throws me down to the floor. My kneecap makes this snapping sound, but when she walks away (she's alone) I try to stand up and I can. So it's okay.

And Bianca needs me, so it's okay. It's okay.

So I'm pretty sure what Mason meant by "game changer" wasn't James's parents finding out about Ian and threatening to send him away to *military school* (and hello there, empty threats, because where's that money coming from, exactly?) but, you know, surprise.

I don't get the full story out of Bianca of how it happened. Maybe James wasn't quiet enough on the phone. Maybe his parents checked his texts. All I know, absolutely, unequivocally, is that Bianca didn't tell them, and that on some level she's furious at James and she doesn't know *why* and it's because he shattered your damn world, sweetheart. He didn't do anything wrong but neither did you and you are fourteen.

Bianca is crying in my car that this is the worst thing that could ever happen to them, that James is a mess, that how dare her parents be such bigoted assholes (she says "assholes") and how could James be so stupid and how could she be so *stupid* and she is sobbing herself hoarse. And Bee, God, and I know, of all the things to care about, shut up, Etta, but she's screwing up her throat and our audition is in two days.

I drop her off at her house and her parents' car is gone, but James comes and meets us at the car. He's scuffing his feet, barely says hi to me. He looks more like Bianca than he ever has.

I hug her and him and leave them there, and when I look back as I'm pulling away, they are sobbing and screaming at each other.

The second round of auditions is for a whole bunch of Midwesterners, and it's in Kansas City. Mason said anyone even a little east of us is probably going to Chicago, but I'm just glad we don't have to drive that far for a low-rent New York, sorry I'm not sorry.

Still, it's a four-hour drive, so Bianca decides to sleep over the night before so we can get an early start on it and so she can just get away from everything. She's a mess still, shaky, and having her in my house is this stressful balancing act. I told my mom not to bother her about food, that yeah, we get it, she's really skinny, it's a problem, we get her to eat when we can, just please, please don't get involved. My mom hugged me, really tight, which I wasn't expecting, and she let me and Bianca have dinner in the dining room, where she and Kristina couldn't watch us. Bianca didn't eat.

We change into pajamas pretty immediately after dinner because why the hell not, and then we go up to my attic and I put on my toe shoes.

"Do something," she says. She's still hoarse. I keep telling her not to talk. "Anything."

I turn some fouettés because they were always my favorites and because they feel like sinking into a bubble bath.

"I missed this so much," I say. "I just, I missed this *so* much."

And then I'm dancing. The floorboards are creaking underneath me but I don't care. I'm doing the *Swan Lake* combinations I memorized back when I was this tiny kid twirling in front of the TV when I watched the grainy VHS recording my mom made for the billionth time. I'm this baby in her shoes at her first class and I'm the sixteen-year-old who really genuinely loved this until one teacher made her feel like shit and apparently that was all it took to convince her that ballet wanted her to be small.

Ballet wants me to be big, to be sweeping lines (but my body isn't lines, I don't *understand*) to be committed with every inch of me, and however many inches I have, I can do it.

Ballet.

Maybe my first best friend. It can fight Rachel for the title. (It can fight Rachel for everything, I guess.)

Bianca's entranced, knees up to her chin.

"You're beautiful," she says.

I smile at her and cool down through some pliés and slow stretching. "You should do ballet."

"I trip over my feet *walking*." She lies down, cheek against the floor. "And I get so tired now."

"I know, baby."

"If you don't get into Brentwood, you should try for dancing schools. Aren't there big ones in New York?"

"Yeah, but I don't really do ballet anymore. I don't know if I want to. I want . . ." God. I want this girl, or I want people who are going to make me feel like this girl does. I want people with big voices who surprise me and scare me and make me feel things and I want this girl to not wilt and die like this is a Victorian novel.

I think she's falling asleep here.

"I have a better shot at them, though, I guess," I say.

"Maybe." She yawns.

I say, "You've got to get better, Bee."

"I know."

"This . . . what you're doing. This isn't sustainable."

"I don't want to do this anymore."

"That's big, you know?"

She shrugs. "Except I don't know anything else I want to do either."

"You want to sing."

She shrugs again, closing her eyes. "I'm so tired."

I wake up at seven to a motorcycle roaring outside, and, genuine surprise, Mason's here, and, bigger surprise, he has James.

"This kid is not missing his audition," Mason says.

I run up to James and hug him. "What about Ian?"

"He's meeting us there," Mason says, and I let James go so Bianca can get all over him, asking if he's okay and checking him over like their parents might have hit him (shit they wouldn't hit him, would they?). Mason knows I'm thinking it and he catches my eye and shakes his head all reassuring. Okay.

"I'm fine, Bee," James says. "Stop fussing. C'mere." He gathers her all up and kisses her forehead. "Hey, you're shivering."

"She's gonna have a yogurt shake in the car," I say. "Right, Bianca?"

"Uh-huh."

"Park the motorcycle in the garage," I say to Mason. I kiss him quickly on his way by. "And get in the car. We have to go."

I drive most of the way, with Mason taking shifts, and Bianca and James crash in the backseat together. They're not saying much, just leaning all over each other, and when they do talk it's too quietly for me to hear most of it. But the gist is that their parents are threatening all kinds of ship-you-off-to-military-school bullshit and Bianca's freaking out.

"You didn't do anything wrong," I hear her say at some point, and God, this is so like when Mom went to that PTA meeting and some parent said some homophobic bullshit and my mom came home and hugged me and told me how proud of me she was and how she didn't care who I wanted to love, all of that stuff. I guess there's nothing like someone in front of you being an actual bigot to make you climb out of your own hardwired bullshit. It's not Bianca's fault she's got this under-pinning of prejudice, y'know? I should really forgive my mom, too, but there's got to be a difference between Bianca's hesi-tation to let James date a guy and my mom's hesitation with me, first of all because Bianca's issues are religious while my mom's are just *this isn't how things have been done*, and second of all because I'm her daughter and supporting me is her *job*, isn't it? I mean, I'm not out killing people, I'm just making out with girls, and if she didn't want to have to deal with me then she should have thought of that before she got pregnant. I'm fundamentally a good kid. I know that.

Sometimes.

Anyway, somehow this all culminates in me calling Rachel at a rest stop.

"God, what fucking decade is this?" she says.

I'm still trying to get over the fact that she answered, and now I have to warp my brain until I've processed that yes, I did just tell her all about James's issues with Ian and their parents and yes, I somehow did it all without revealing that there's nothing going on with Bianca and yes, I've somehow acciden-tally become a terrible and manipulative person. No wonder my mom judges me.

I say, "I don't even know how to deal with this. Every time our parents were shitty they were, like, sane-people shitty."

"Right? Are they going to send him to one of those repro-gramming camps?"

"What? No. I don't think anyone actually does that. Wait, do people do that?"

"I think they use electroshock there."

"You know some people—"

"Find electroshock very helpful and the way the media portrays it as a torture form isn't accurate since it's still thera-peutically safe and effective for many cases. You're so predict-able, Ett."

"Well, you know how I love to be up-to-date on treatments of homosexuality."

"When is someone going to suggest weed as a cure, that's what I want to know."

I miss her.

She says, "Ugh, I've got to go."

"Going out?"

"What? It's nine thirty, you're lucky *I'm* awake, you think the other Dykes are?"

"Right."

"I'm taking the twins to the park."

That sounds like some kind of strange euphemism. "Tell them Aunt Etta says hi." I'm really pushing my luck here.

"I will," she says. She pauses. Then, "Let's have lunch when you get back? Break a leg."

So that's it, then. We're going to be okay. Rachel isn't a bad person. Rachel isn't James's parents in this metaphor, maybe wanting to send me to reprogramming camp because I slept with a guy. Rachel's just this girl, just my best friend, trying to reevaluate how she thinks of me because I did something she wasn't expecting. It doesn't have to be the political move the Dykes are trying to make it. Maybe they really care if I'm a lesbian, maybe they were just looking for a coup or were bored and wanted some drama. Rachel doesn't care that I'm not a lesbian. Rachel cares that I'm not the girl who she thought I was.

And maybe I'm not. I don't really know what girl I am. I'll figure it out. Maybe with her.

18

THE AUDITION HALLWAY LOOKS ABOUT THE SAME AS THE OTHER, just with a ton more people. The list of who got through last round was only about twenty people from *all* of Nebraska, and here we are with the deserted half of the Midwest, let's be honest, and there's still more people here than I bet are in the entire student body of Brentwood, so unless they're looking to totally clear the decks there, just about all of us are screwed. I always knew I didn't have a prayer, but now I'm looking at crazy-talented James and Bianca and thinking they might not either. Maybe Bianca was in better shape emotionally, if not physically, when she tried out last year. But she did it once. She can do it again. She deserves this. Be big, Bee.

There's an acting section of this audition, a cold reading, always Shakespeare, James says, but nobody knows what it is.

Probably shitty for girls. Guys get all the good monologues in Shakespeare. And pretty much in everything. There's also a dance combination, turns out, maybe a little harder than last time, and then whatever we want to sing—a short section, twenty-four to forty-eight bars, and mine is right at the long end of that because I have to get as much Sheila in as I can to develop that personality and have even the tiniest prayer, and I'm really concerned that that's going to count against me. Bianca, James, and Ian are all prepared at this point and here I am bouncing from foot to foot like I have toe shoes on.

Oh and did I mention it's a cappella? As in no music? Jesus Christ.

"Maybe I can just go in there and dance," I say to Bianca. "They're like, 'Etta, come sing,' and I'm like *nope* and just start dancing."

"Calm down," she says, but she's jittery as hell too, shaking down to the ends of her fingers. At least she drank that yogurt shake, but now she's all worried about how that might have affected her throat, which is still sore.

"I can't do this," she says, all of a sudden.

"What?"

"This is too much. Just . . . I can't *concentrate*. This is too much, I can't do this, I'm going to mess up."

"Bianca. Hey."

"I'm going to screw it up and they're going to be *laughing* at me."

"Look at me, Bianca."

She does. Her chin's shaking.

I lower my voice to the damn ground. "You're better than all of these people and you know it. You can do this."

"I'm scared."

"I know. I'll be right there with you."

"I'm going to mess up. I know it."

"I'll be right there."

We take these deep breaths and kind of hold on to each other and then it's time to go.

The dance combination is still easy, but there are more girls struggling this time, so I guess it's not as easy as the last one. Bianca isn't perfect but she's been practicing steps with me so she's better than a lot of them.

The monologue is Juliet. All righty then, way to dig deep, auditioners. A bunch of the girls are really, really good. Once again I'm called near the end of it, so I just sit here and drive myself crazy reading it over and over and rating the other girls from one to ten. Bianca's a seven. It'll do, I think, once they hear her sing. But she's shaky, and that's not good. They're not going to like that. And she doesn't do anything the other girls didn't do, but at least she does it well.

Then it's my turn and I'm thinking, *well, it worked for "Far from the Home I Love," and these are different people so maybe they don't know all my tricks.* Worth a shot.

At least it's not the balcony monologue. It's Juliet coming

up with her plan to drink the poison that will make everyone think she's dead blah blah yeah yeah. *Romeo and Juliet* is stupid, but this is probably the best part. The other girls are playing the monologue fairly straight, which for Shakespeare means exaggerated, and I get that, and naturally it would be the choice I would make, but I have to be weird so here goes.

I step up and take a deep breath and yep, let's do this.

> *Farewell! God knows when we shall meet again.*
> *I have a faint cold fear thrills through my veins,*
> *That almost freezes up the heat of life:*
> *I'll call them back again to comfort me:*
> *Nurse! What should she do here?*
> *My dismal scene I needs must act alone.*
> *Come, vial.*

And so on and so forth. Instead of trying to disguise when I'm looking down at my paper, I make it part of the monologue, and instead of being all tragic and romantic I'm doing it like a crazy person, mumbling to myself, and instead of asking questions to the audience I'm asking them to the voices in my head or whatever. I'm just muttering these lines, and maybe you can't understand them all but come on, they've already listened to it through twenty-five girls, and then I'm saying some of them loud, bold, but not the ones you would expect. I'm punctuating weird spots and pausing in weird places and saying some of it as straight and clear as a seventeen-year-old modern damn girl, because I'm not a fourteen-year-old tragic heroine and in a minute I'm going to pretend to be some thirty-five-year-old washed up dancer in "At the Ballet" so if I want to be Etta for any of this (I was dancing in the second row to the side; they couldn't see *me*, just a girl who got all the steps right) then I have to do it right now. So screw it. These other girls could be a real Juliet better than I could anyway, so if this doesn't work at least I did what I could.

None of these girls except Bianca heard me do a bizarre rendition of "Far from the Home I Love" like the same one-trick pony I apparently am, so they're all looking at me like I'm crazy all anew just like those girls did. I'm choosing to believe that's a good sign because hey, it worked once, and Bianca's smiling at me.

And then it's singing time.

They go reverse-order this time so I'm near the beginning. I've practiced this a hundred times, so even if I know it's far from perfect, it's not especially scary. I focus on getting the character through and *not* making it look like I've done it a hundred damn times.

And when I get to the chorus I sing a few of the notes as pretty and clear as I can to show that I have at least *some* skill, that I can do more than talk my way through a song that's conveniently meant to be talked through. What's weird is that I do pretty well on showing off those couple of notes. I only have to sing a little bit, all in all, so as long as they don't clock me on that I'm pretty sure I got through it, and it's not like I didn't do the song how it's supposed to be done. All they can judge me for is my song choice, and, you know, fair enough, but just like the monologue this is about all I can do. I can't hold a whole song on my own like Bianca. I can't hit the high note in Maggie's part of "At the Ballet," so I'll just be Sheila and I'll do a damn good job.

Unlike the confused silence after my monologue, I get some applause now, hooray.

Some other girls go, and I'm actually surprised by how just okay some of them are. Don't get me wrong, there's a ton of talent here, but in between there are girls who I'm kind of wondering how they got through. I mean, they're no worse than me (except this one girl, did she sleep with someone?) but they didn't choose the right song for them. Like, come on, don't try to sing "It Won't Be Long Now" if you can't fly your way into Vanessa's high notes, y'know?

And then it's Bianca, and God, she's nervous in this way she's only supposed to be for the dancing. I give her wrist a little squeeze on her way up to the front of the room. She can do this. She's auditioned with "Let's Hear It for the Boy" a billion times. I realize all of a sudden that there's a good chance these exact auditioners have heard her do "Let's Hear It for the Boy" a billion times and maybe they'll remember her as the girl they once let in or maybe they'll take off points for that maybe being the only song she can sing. But it isn't. Bianca could sing *anything*.

But she doesn't. She's afraid.

So she sings it, and she sings it well. She hits her notes and gets her vibrato on the right ones. But she doesn't sing it like she's having fun. She doesn't sing it with that spark in her. She doesn't sing like it's easy and she wants it and she's pouring out notes like water.

She doesn't sing it like *Bianca*.

And I know in that minute that she's screwed.

Called back:

James Grey
a really small group of people we don't care about
Me

19

ME.

Who the hell have I fooled?

The list is posted online somewhere between fifth and sixth period and I see it when I've run to the computer lab to check, and there it is, there it freaking is, fifty names from all over the country and one of them is James and one of them is *me*. In two weeks they're flying us into New York to meet with the board and sing and dance and read all by ourselves for the final audition.

And one of them is *me*.

And none of them is Bianca.

I know at some point I need to call her, or maybe James first, but I can't. My phone immediately lights up with texts from Mason. *Congrats!!* and *dinner tonight?* but I can't, I can't, because I don't know how many spots they're looking to fill but I know that, on some level, it could have been Bianca and not me. They could have taken me out and put her in.

And I know there is a part of me that does want to call and convince them to switch her in for me.

And there is a part of me that *doesn't*.

So no, I can't call her right now. I can't do anything but duck into the nearest bathroom and bawl, and I didn't even process what time it is or what floor I'm on and then I hear that voice, all feathers and cream and *home*, saying, "Etta?"

I sink to the floor of my stall and I'm crying so hard I can't see her, but then she crawls under the door of the stall and unlocks it and she's sitting with me and she says, "Shh shh shh okay, come here. Etta, it's okay, hey hey hey."

I hear the bathroom door open and someone says, "Rachel?" I think it's Isabel.

"Fuck off, okay?" Rachel says.

"Jesus, fine." The door closes.

Rachel pulls me into her, crossing her legs over mine, whispering, "Okay, okay. Did they do something?" she says. "I told them to leave you alone, honey, I told them . . ."

"I'm a terrible friend, I'm a terrible friend, I'm a terrible goddamn friend."

"No. Hey. No, you're not."

"Y-yes."

"No. And come on, who would know better than me."

I sniffle and hide in the collar of her expensive coat and God, it's so familiar, this is so safe, why did I ever want to go to New York when this girl was right here, I need to call and convince them to switch Bianca in for me, I need to make all of this right, I can fix this, I can *fix* this. If Rachel's holding me I can fix anything.

"Is this about Cupcake?" she says.

"What?"

"You didn't hear."

"Rachel, what?"

"Come on," she says. "Screw Spanish. You need something chocolate."

We're at the retro coffee shop. She buys me hot chocolate and gets just tea for herself. They're out of caramel apple lattes. Being best friends with a diabetic was always such a mindfuck for a wannabe anorexic, but it's not like diabetics can't eat sugar, they just have to shoot up extra for it, so she'd use it as a card to play sometimes, *look, if I can eat a cookie so can you.*

"So tell me what happened," she says.

"We went to the audition and we'd prepared so hard, all three of us. I didn't hear the boys audition and I've never heard Ian sing so I don't know, maybe he wasn't that good, but he got through to the second round so he couldn't have been awful but then again so did I and how did I make it to *third*—"

"Slow down. Who's Ian?"

"James's boyfriend."

"And James is . . ."

"Bianca's brother. He's my friend."

Old Rachel would have teased me, *you're friends with a boy? Do you know where their hands have been?* Especially a gay boy. All that *Queer as Folk* bullshit about lesbians and gay boys being friends is, yeah, bullshit. We dance at the same clubs and that's about it.

Except apparently not even that, because Cupcake's closing down. They're shutting down the whole strip. Health code violations, noise complaints, crime, gay gay gay gay gay.

I pause and say, "I can't believe that. Cupcake was the only decent thing around here."

"Right? I don't even know what's going to happen now. We'll have to found our own club. One with an actual liquor bar." She's coughing out this laugh, but she's red under the eyes and I think maybe she's been crying about Cupcake, and that makes me wonder, comparatively, how much she's cried about me.

"Hey," Rachel says. "Keep talking."

"About Bianca?"

"Uh-huh."

"She's amazing, and she wasn't even *bad*, not even *sort of*, she just wasn't good *enough*. She just wasn't fucking *perfect* and like what do I do with that, we're trying to convince this girl that she can eat, that she doesn't have to be this delicate little thing, that she doesn't have to be *perfect*, and then here she is and she blew everything because she had *one* off day, how am I supposed to expect her to eat a freaking sandwich now?"

"You really love her, huh?" Rachel says, and I really don't care that she doesn't mean it the way I do because it doesn't matter.

"I really, really do."

"And you don't want to do this, do you? Brentwood. Not really."

I didn't say that part, but maybe she's right.

"Come on," she says. "Theater school? What happened to math?"

"I know."

"I thought you wanted to be a teacher." It's that voice again, that *I thought I knew you.*

I wanted to be a dance teacher. "I do, I just . . ."

"You want to do this first?"

I nod a little.

She says, "You'll get in. I know you will."

"I don't know how I've gotten through this far. It doesn't make sense."

"They see something in you. Come on, don't look so surprised. So maybe you're not the best of all of them, but you're a star, Etta. You've got a drive in you other people just don't."

"I don't know."

"If you could spend a day as someone else, you would. Nobody else cares about things like you do. Nobody sets their mind to stuff and just gets it done. You're the only person I know who can get an A on a test just because she decides she's going to."

I mean, I decide I'm going to and then decide to study for three hours a night the week before the test—there's no magic going on here, you know?—but I know what she means. And I like it, even if I don't know if I believe her. I'm *just* Etta.

I was just named after a damn musical goddess, I know, I know, and I really need to go call my other half.

She says, "I just . . . you know."

I don't know. "What?"

"Don't want you to go."

"Oh . . ."

"No, I know it's stupid and selfish, it's just . . . I don't know. I feel like we're fixing us, you know?"

I nod, even though I'm not sure, because this feels too much like I'm making a new friend and not enough like I'm falling back into what we had. Right now I can't imagine going home with Rachel and baking cookies for her sisters and falling asleep watching *Paris Is Burning*. I feel like those things happened in another life.

"I started ballet again," I say, even though it's (maybe) not technically true, just as a test of some kind, I guess.

Her face is neutral. "Yeah?" she says. "Why?"

"Because I felt like if I didn't I would die, or something," I say, which is a quote from *My So-Called Life*, which we devoured when we were in fourth grade. We thought we would be Angela and Rayanne. We thought we would have them make up in the finale and grow old together. We would have so much more than one season.

She cracks a smile.

Maybe this means something. Maybe this means I can really do ballet again. God, I shouldn't need her approval for it. I don't know.

"You should come out with us tonight," she says. "Cupcake's open another week. We're doing this big push-the-boat-out party."

"We?"

She crosses her ankles with a shrug. She never looks at home in this uniform. She should be in her flare-leg jeans, her hippy-dippy headbands, her white eyeliner. No, she should be in her T-shirt and yoga pants like she was in middle school, before we knew the Disco Dykes existed. She should be in the crap I wear now because it's all that fits.

If it were a movie, I'd dump Rachel like she dumped me and find a hot guy and make out on her car. I mean, I would get Mason to make out on her car with me. It's kind of weird that my mind didn't immediately go to him, I guess.

I was supposed to have dinner with him tonight. And I know I'm supposed to see Bianca.

"I'll talk to them," she says. "If I tell them to be cool, they'll be cool. Or I'll just get them really drunk first, whatever."

"Can we get really drunk first? Like, now?"

She checks her watch. "It's Tuesday?"

"Uh-huh. Your mom works late. Twins have gymnastics."

"Yep. Yes. We can get really drunk first like now."

20

RACHEL BARELY DRINKS BECAUSE HER BLOOD SUGAR TANKS, SO
pretty much we're just cashed out on her bathroom floor with
some bottle of wine she produces from her parents' cellar and
she's had two sips and I've had a zillion and she's giggly because
I'm giggly or I'm giggly because she's giggly and we are lying
on the rug where she taught me how to play Jenga when I
was five and taught me how to have an orgasm when I was
fifteen and I just love her. I fell in love and fell inside of this
girl, forever, and maybe this is what I wanted this whole time.
Not Danielle. Not Brentwood. Not New York, not Bianca, not
skinny or happy or ballet or healthy, just *home*. This rug, and
a lot of wine, and Rachel.

"Rachel," I say. "Rachel, we've gotta . . . be us."

"Aw, we are, sweetie," she says. That doesn't sound right. "We will be."

"You got it. You *got* it." I curl up with my head on her knee and she braids some of my dreadlocks. "What if I go to New York?"

She laughs a little. "Remember when we used to make plans?" In our PSAT prep class—we have the exact same type of mother, I swear—we would sit in the back in our hip-huggers and platforms that were somehow so *sad* when we were in that community center and look at the printouts from the practice tests they gave us and the scores that never got higher and never got lower no matter what we did, whether we studied or cried or took them flat-out stoned, and we memorized bus schedules and wrote them in the front of each other's study books, and she wanted to go to Chicago but I wanted to go to New York and for the first time in our entire lives she gave in and let me win because I wanted it *so much* (God, that was the first time, that was the only time, this is my best friend) and we wrote maps to bus stations and maps for Manhattan subways and maps to where our parents hid their credit cards, and we knew we were never going to do it and that made us want to do it so much more, and shit, we're not fifteen anymore, I might be actually going, I could drop out of this audition and go to New York with Rachel and I wouldn't be stealing Bianca's dream and maybe we'd bring Bianca with us because Rachel would *love* her and we could work in coffeehouses and Bianca could sing in subway stations and we'd save up and send her to Brentwood and I would find Danielle or I would marry Rachel because she is beautiful and she gives me wine and everything would be beautiful and perfect forever.

"I remember," I say.

"We were so crazy."

"We should do it."

She laughs, kisses my forehead. She's so warm. "Yeah?"

"Uh-huh. You and me. I'm not gonna get into the school. Someone else should get into the school."

"You could look at ballet schools."

I sit up so fast I almost hit her in the chin. Rachel told me to go to ballet school. *Rachel thinks I should do ballet.* Rachel sees me and a bun and leotard and sees me being a real ballerina with white girls six inches taller and thirty pounds less than me and Rachel thinks I wouldn't be caving to the masculine hierarchy and Rachel *understands me and Rachel loves me so much and I should go to ballet school.* I should go to ballet school and Rachel will love me and I will be dancing and Brentwood has its generic and sad little dance program and there are ballet schools and somebody—*Rachel*—thinks that I could do it.

I am beautiful at the ballet.

"Please, Ray."

"What about school for me?"

"Rachel, you can go to a magnet program and you can

go to med school and you can be a doctor and we can be Bohemians and you can be a Bohemian doctor."

She's laughing still, head tipped back, beautiful. "That does sound pretty perfect."

"Let's do it. Let's *do* it."

"What was the plan? Greyhound?"

"Yes, Rachel, but the Omaha Greyhound station closed down—*I know right*—but there is a Burlington Trailways stop there and all we have to do is get to like Omaha and then it's like a hundred and eighty dollars apiece! And then we get to New York and we can live in Washington Heights which is scary but I'm black so I can pretend I'm all hardcore and shit! And then go to ballet school, haha fooled them!"

"When would we leave?"

"Right *now!*"

"What about the big farewell to Cupcake!"

"New York will be our farewell to Cupcake! Farewell to damn *NEBRASKA!*" My phone's ringing. "Hang on."

"Come pick me up," Bianca says, no introduction. I'm beginning to think this is how she says hello. I get off Rachel's lap and sober up a little, but so not enough to drive.

"Are you okay?"

"Pick me *up.*"

I lower the phone and say, "Can you drive me some-where?"

She finds her keys. "Where?"

"Get Bianca."

"Is she coming out with us?"

"Um. Probably not."

"Then what are we gonna do with her?"

"I have no idea. But she needs me."

Rachel blows air out of her mouth. "All right, babe. Let's do this."

In the car I dodge another call from Mason—seriously, take a hint, you're not my boyfriend in general and you definitely are not tonight—and drive to Bianca's house. She's out the door before we've even turned off the car.

I say, "Bianca, this is Rachel."

"She's the nice one?"

"Yeah."

"Hi, Rachel."

"Hey there, Bianca."

I say, "Want to go back to my house? We can make cookie dough and watch *Cabaret*."

Rachel whines, and Bianca shakes her head.

"Just *Cabaret*, no cookie dough?"

Another head shake.

"Coffee? Irish pub? Want to see what Mason's up to?"

"Who's Mason?" Rachel says.

"Friend of hers. Shh." But Bianca's still shaking her head, and shit, what else can we do that has nothing to do with these auditions? Can I drink more? I want to drink more.

"Want to go to the park and sit on the swings? I'll push you."

"No. I want to go *out*."

"Technically all of those were . . . are you drunk?"

I expect her to laugh at me, tell me she's just *tired*, just *happy*, just *fourteen*.

"I'm not *drunk*," she says, but she's not laughing. "I just have *been drinking*."

"Holy shit, Bee."

"How come in books and stuff parents always lock the liquor cabinet? Who locks a liquor cabinet?"

"Whoa. Okay. Yeah, we're going back to my house." I can't bring her back to her house like this. It's a miracle her parents hadn't noticed already. We're not going to push our luck.

Rachel says, "What about Cupcake?"

"Rachel . . ."

"Fine," Bianca says. "Might as well go home," she says, though. "Like my parents give a shit around telling Jamie 'no way you'll go to New York, New York is full of faggots.'"

"I don't think I like your parents," Rachel says.

"I don't think I like fucking *anything*."

"Bianca."

"I want to go ouuuut! Take me somewhere. Take me anywhere." She rests her head on my shoulder. "Let's go ooooout."

"There is no way I'm taking you anywhere," I say.

Rachel says, "Ettaaaa?"

"What."

"If she's gonna go out anyway, might as well be where she won't be alone, right? Might as well be full of fags to piss her parents off?"

"No way."

But Bianca's sitting up all straight in the backseat. "Yes! Take me out. I like Rachel."

The stupid thing is that I *know* this is a bad idea. I just can't think of a better one.

And maybe a night with some lesbians will be enough to steer her back toward the straight (pun not intended, or, you know, maybe, she is drunk and with a drunk bisexual right now) and narrow.

But still. "I'm going to call James, okay?"

She says, "James isn't at home."

"What? Where is he?"

"*Counseling.*"

"Jesus, your parents are big on counseling."

"Yes."

"My mom's with him. Crying the gay away.'"

"Shit. All right." So she's mine tonight. Okay. Rachel's all animated, telling Bianca how much fun we're gonna have, and it's about time she meets some of *her own kind*. God, Rachel thinks they're a two-gay family, shit shit shit, this is going to end so poorly and I can't even see *how* because there are just way too many fucking ways this could be a disaster and I don't even know which ones are the most likely because I'm half-drunk and I really wish I were full-drunk right this damn minute.

I actually end up texting James as soon as we pull up to Rachel's house. *ive got her tonight*

thank you

Okay.

We sit in Rachel's bathroom and put on makeup, and Rachel's dressing up Bianca like she's a little doll, pinning miniskirts and tying up T-shirts so they fit her tiny body. She mother-hens all over her while she does it.

"You don't need to be this skinny to be beautiful," she says, as if being beautiful is the point. There's a part of this that lay-people are just never, ever going to get.

I snatch a water bottle of totally not-water away from Bianca when I see her taking a sip. "No. You've had more than enough." I shrug and drink it myself, whatever, I'm not driving, and if I'm facing the Dykes tonight I'm going to need it. I can't believe *this* is the way it's going full circle from the night three months ago when I tried to corner them. I'm going back to Cupcake with Rachel and *Bianca* flanking me. How did this happen?

Rachel's putting up Bianca's hair and talking all softly into her ear, and Bianca's giggling and squirming because she's drunk and has no idea she's being flirted with. I don't know why it's bothering me. Rachel's always done this with girls I'm with, and I've always done it with girls she's with. It doesn't mean anything, not about them, anyway. I guess it's just a way of asserting our ownership—*I can do whatever I want to you because at the end of the night I'm the one going home with her. At the end of the whole world, I'm the one going home with her.*

I don't know what I was thinking, really, having Bianca and Rachel in the same room. I just want to go to Cupcake and get wasted like the old days or wrap Bianca up in her coat and take her home like the new days, and why why why is my brain defaulting to those options and not movie nights with Rachel, motorcycle rides with James and Bianca and Mason and—God, Ian, why the hell not? Why don't I ever think of the parts of both of my lives that I've actually *liked*?

Because I don't like babying Bianca. I don't.

I like singing with Bianca.

I like laughing with Bianca.

I like getting better with Bianca.

I thought this wouldn't wear me down. I thought I could keep taking care of her forever and that I was strong and it wouldn't drag me down.

I think maybe I was an idiot.

I know that I'm a terrible damn friend.

"Etta should sing for us," Bianca says. She's on the floor now, leaning her head against Rachel's laundry hamper.

I say, "I'll sing if you eat something."

She pouts but nibbles on the crackers Rachel brings her.

So I climb up onto the hamper, bothering her foot with

my sock some just for good measure, and belt out the entirety of "At the Ballet," which is ridiculous because I'm trying to do three parts at once, and Bianca helps me with the harmonies at some points, so quietly that I don't know if she knows she's doing it (would she sing right now if she knew? Has that been ruined for her?) but it's still this ridiculous mess of me trying to do all the parts. And then I get to Maggie's part, Maggie's monologue about dancing around the living room with her arms up like this, and it's hard to keep going.

I make some excuse about not knowing this part as well, when really I know it a zillion times better than Bebe's (that's the second girl, I looked it up eventually) because lately when I'm supposed to sing Sheila's part I find myself singing Maggie's instead, which is stupid because I can't hit the high notes and you need this *sincerity* to be Maggie anyway, and how am I supposed to go into an audition for a place I don't even know that I want (can I just audition for a freaking city, can Bianca go to Brentwood and we'll do brunch every day) and act sincere? No, I can be brassy and loud and not sing all that well.

But they make me keep going, so I sing out Maggie's three "at the ballet!"s, each one going higher and higher, and hey, big shock, I can't hit the highest note.

But I got the first two, and that's new.

The girls are just chuckling a little. "Yeah," Rachel says, "Stick to the first part."

"I know," I say. "I was going to."

She raises an eyebrow. "Don't get attitudey with me. What's the matter?"

"I don't know. Eat your crackers, Bianca."

"I am," she says, and she is. "Where are we going?"

"Club Cupcake." Rachel finishes her mascara, blinks in the mirror. "On the strip."

"The *gay* strip?" Bianca's all excited.

Rachel laughs. "Yeah, honey. Before they shut it down and ruin whatever Nebraska once had."

I say, "Ease her into this, okay?"

Rachel says, "What, like a bunch of lesbians are going to be all that new to her? Maybe a bunch of lesbians and some loud music, that's fair."

Jesus, I have got to find a chance to get Rachel alone and tell her that Bianca is so, so not gay. Bianca leans on me because she *knows* I know she's not gay. The second she thinks I'm trying to pull her into this I become not safe to her and that's going to scare the shit out of her, because right now I am her bridge between her and her brother and I get that, and that's fine, but that doesn't mean she should go swimming underneath me and getting all wet, you know? God, that wasn't even supposed to sound dirty.

So I just say, "She's young and she's drunk. Go easy."

Rachel turns on me, all of a sudden all sharp lines and painted lips. "What exactly do you think I'm going to do to her, Etta?"

God, this is a shitshow. I take another swallow from the bottle. What is this, Everclear? All of a sudden I'm all emotional thinking about when I was Bianca's age and I had to go to the hospital for alcohol poisoning after some sweet sixteen for this junior-year Dyke. I'm all weepy looking at Bianca on the floor with her crackers and yeah, this shit is strong and Rachel's shoulder is warm under my cheek.

She kisses the top of my head and dabs a little more blush onto my cheeks. "All right. Let's get moving. Etta, you want the tie-dye coat?"

I do. I do want the tie-dye coat.

Rachel wraps a headband around Bianca's forehead. "Let's go."

Cupcake is louder than I remembered and somehow gayer, and maybe that's because everyone knows they've got a limited time left or maybe it's because my gay experiences of late have been domestic little James and Ian and I'd forgotten about this other end of the spectrum, the glittiest glitter that has ever glittered, this was my life, these shirtless boys with their mouths on each other. I used to love this. I used to genuinely love this, and not in some damaged daddy-left-us-so-now-I-sleep-around way. I just *liked* it.

And now Bianca's clinging to me and I feel protective and guilty as hell, and why do I feel guilty, she wanted to come, I'm not her mother and there's nothing *wrong* with a goddamn gay club, so what if I had to flirt a little with the door Dyke to get Bianca in, it's not like she doesn't have Xs on her hands so she can't drink any more. (But it's also not like they're being very careful about who drinks because what does Cupcake have to be afraid of at this point, I know the feeling.) Maybe I just think that I've found something bigger for the same reason I thought I liked ballet (do I like ballet? I can't remember). Something about the patriarchy. I'm dizzy.

I bring Bianca to the armchairs where I found the Dykes the last time I was here and put her in one. "Stay."

"I want to dance!"

"I'll dance with you soon, I promise. But I have to take care of some stuff first."

"Are those the Dykes?" she says, like they're celebrities. Drunk girl.

"Don't worry about it, sweetie." I give her a kiss on the cheek and try to convince myself it isn't because I know Rachel's watching. Bianca hums contentedly and puts her head back. Okay.

I swim through the crowd to Rachel and there's the trifecta, matching maxi dresses tonight, aren't we adorable. Isabel must have made them. She made us all T-shirts one time but mine was too small and I still don't know if it was on purpose or not. God, why were these girls my friends? Everything is *so* clear now. Everything is fantastic! I don't have to be friends with them and I don't have to do this audition and I don't have to fix Bianca! I can stay here and dance by myself forever and ever, yaaay I love alcohol. I don't think I realized how much shit was weighing me down until *right now* when it's gone. I'm a free bird with a mezzo-soprano voice and a big ass and I am dancing around like it is springtime.

Natasha's staring at me either like I'm disgusting or like she can't believe I'm here or maybe both, but Isabel and Titania are smiling a little like maybe they're over all this bullshit. Okay, Isabel and Titania, you can stay.

We like *Etta. Etta can stay.* That was James! I should call him. I love James. Rachel gives me the rest of her drink.

I grab Isabel's hand and say, "Dance with me!" because what the hell, Isabel is so boring and maybe we can loosen her up. I've always kind of liked her, though. She's nice to my sister. I wonder what's going on with my sister. I bet Rachel knows. She hugged her. "What's going on with my sister?"

"What?" Isabel says.

"I wasn't talking to you! Rachel!"

"I can hear you, Etta! Stop yelling."

"The music is *loud*!"

"You're louder!"

"I'm going to mess up my voice!" Oh shit. I can't be *shouting*. I shouldn't be drinking at a club. Why am I doing this? Maybe that's why Rachel wanted me out. Maybe she's trying to sabotage my audition. Maybe this whole thing has been a trick to get me back in so the Dykes can mess with me some more. Maybe they put something in my drink. This is so weird. I'm not high, why am I this paranoid? Where's Bianca? I think maybe I'm paranoid because of Bianca.

Oh right, it doesn't matter if I mess up my voice because I don't care about this audition! Yelling and drinks for everyone! I'm so happy. I lean into Rachel's shoulder. "You're beautiful," I tell her.

"And you are drunk. Mmmm." She squeezes me tight. "I missed you."

"I missed *you!*"

"Let's don't fight again."

"Let's *don't.*"

"Don't go to New York, okay?"

"Okay!"

No. Hey. Wait.

That's not cool.

Why did she just ask me that?

Who does she think she is? She knows how much I want to go to New York. Everyone and their mom knows how much I want to go to New York. What gives her the right to take me out and get me drunk and tell me not to go to New York?

Screw her. Screw Rachel, screw my childhood, where's Bianca? I want to get on a motorcycle. What song is this and why doesn't it have more than four notes? Even I could sing this, come on.

Then I hear Natasha's voice, so close to my ear she doesn't

have to yell. "I can't believe you came here, how fucking stupid can you be?"

"Where's Bianca?" Rachel says.

"That's what I'd like to know!" I probably said that more aggressively than I needed to but it's not my fault I'm having interior monologues about how much I don't like Rachel and that Natasha's pinching me underneath my bra. Wait, why don't I like Rachel? She's tucking one of my dreads behind my ear. She's lovely.

"You are drunk, little girl," she says. She used to call me that. I remember now.

I remember now. "She's in the armchairs. She's over . . ." I turn around. I don't see her. Bee?

"She's adorable," Rachel says. "Even though she's way too skinny."

"She's smoke," I say. "She's blond smoke."

"You can get back into the Dykes!" Rachel says.

"What?"

"Have you guys slept together yet?" she says.

"What?" How have I not told her yet?

"*Have you and Bianca slept together yet?*" she yells over the music, and then over my shoulder someone goes "WHAT?" and yeah, three guesses who that is (Bianca, Bianca, Bianca).

Shit, shit, shit.

"We're not . . . ," I start to say, but I'm so dizzy and she slips away and no no no so I run after her and she's trying to leave but I catch her before she can get to the doors because no no no you are not going out alone, you are just *not*.

"Let *go* of me," she says. She's crying. Oh.

"Bianca."

"You left me to hang out with the *Dykes*?"

Oh God. That's why she's upset.

"Yeah."

"They think we're a *couple*?" Okay, so she's upset about that too.

"They think every two girls is a couple, it doesn't mean anything."

"Why didn't you tell them we aren't?"

"Because—"

"If you're hanging out with these girls who tortured you, if these people who make you feel like shit are your fucking *friends*, then what *am* I? What are we!"

"Bianca. Come to the bathroom or something, okay, we'll talk about this."

"Were you just *using* me?" she says, and holy shit if she thinks that this whole time I've been trying to sleep with her I'm just going to rip out my insides or something, how is it that all I do is tell people what's in my head and I *still* can't get them to know what I'm thinking? I try *so hard*. I want to get better I want to get better I want to *be better* Jesus Christ how many calories are in what Bianca had, how many have we had, how drunk is she?

I should get Rachel to check her blood sugar, it tanks when she drinks—

"I am *not* trying to be something with you," I say. "I don't even think . . . You're not like that in my head. You're like my little sister."

"But you wanted to them to *think* you were?" she says. "You wanted to make them jealous? Why are you hanging out with them?"

"No! Don't you fucking understand? I didn't want to be friends with another damn girl, okay?"

"W-with me?"

"Yes, with you! I never fucking wanted this! I wanted to just put my head down until I got out of here and got to New York and I wanted to hate everyone here and I wanted to hate all girls forever because of what they did to me and I didn't really give a shit if that was unfair because they hurt me *so much*, and then you came along, you just *showed up*, and all I want to do is take care of you and I just want them to love me again okay and you won't do a *thing* to take care of yourself and now how am I supposed to go to New York if you're going to drink and cry and fucking starve yourself to death if I leave you here?"

"So what, you're just gonna be friends with them because they're not going to *die*?"

Oh my God, what is wrong with me. "I don't know, okay? I don't *know*!"

"Fuck you, Etta," she says, and then she pushes through the crowd and weaves her way to the bathroom. Probably to throw up.

I'm a terrible friend.

I am Etta Should Have Stayed Not Otherwise Specified.

I give the bar my fake ID and they ignore the Xs on my hands and give me a beer and then I'm trying to find the Dykes again but it's just Isabel and Titania and Natasha and they don't even look at me and I think maybe they forgot about me and damn it I need to find Rachel I need to find Bianca I need to chug this damn beer.

So I'm pretending to dance with some girls I don't know and they're pretending to dance with me and I'm shaking around in this skirt and I don't even remember whose skirt this is and then someone grabs my arm and I spill my beer all over the floor. "Bianca?" No. It's Rachel.

"Something's wrong," she says. "You need to come with me."

"What? Are you okay?"

"Something's wrong with Bianca."

And it feels like I've been waiting for this sentence my entire life. That I've been dangling on the precipice of that sentence and now I'm falling.

I knew this was going to happen.

I *knew* this was going to happen.

Bianca's on the floor in the bathroom, conscious but limp,

breathing shallow and fast with her head pillowed on her arms. Her eyes are squeezed shut and Rachel says, "Did she drink too much?"

"She didn't . . . She hasn't had anything in hours." I feel her pulse, expecting fast and light, hummingbird, but no, it's so slow.

Her body is breaking.

"I need you to take us to the hospital," I tell Rachel.

For some reason I'm expecting her to say no.

"Absolutely," she says. "I'm gonna run and get the car. I'll text you when I'm pulling up outside, okay?"

How did I think we could be friends again when I thought she would say no to that? How can I keep putting this all on her when I'm the one who doesn't trust her, and I'm not saying she hasn't given me any reasons not to but God, I'm going to need to meet her somewhere in the middle and I don't know if I can do that. I just don't.

This isn't the time to be thinking about this because Bianca is floppy against my chest, and I'm just holding her and holding her.

"Can you carry her?" Rachel says.

"Uh-huh. Go go go."

Rachel's gone, and people are coming and going in the bathroom and tripping over us and not stopping to see if we need help. I hate everybody but this girl. I tuck her in under my chin. She's shivering now.

"E-Etta."

"Shh shh shh. I know."

"Leave me alone."

Yeah, whatever. She's fourteen.

But it still hurts.

"I'm not going anywhere." I kiss the top of her head. "I love you, baby girl. You're going to be just fine, we're gonna get you some help, okay?"

"I don't want help—mychesthurts."

"I know. Hang in there."

"I want *Jamie*."

"I know. I know I'm gonna get him, I'll get him, please just hold on, okay, Rachel's coming, we're gonna go, I'm gonna fix this."

She's crying, and she has stopped pulling away. She's gripping me around the waist, shaking so hard I feel like she's going to fall into pieces.

"Gonna fix you," I tell her. "Hang in there, you hear me? Hang in there."

21

I GUESS THIS IS ENOUGH OF A CRISIS TO MAKE JAMES'S PARENTS forget that they hate him, because all three of them show up at the hospital bedraggled and together, in pajamas because I guess Christians go to bed before eleven, like my mom. I wish my mom were here. It's just me and Rachel, who's lingering by the coffee machine, making tea for me, all of that. I don't know what to say to her. I don't know what to say to anybody. I made sure Bianca was settled in her bed and that they were getting her fluids and she was going to be okay and then I came out here and I sat in this chair where I can see into her room (she's sedated but still trying to pull out her IV, I think she knows there's sugar in it) and I'm just planted here, I can't move. I wish this somehow magically sobered me up, but that doesn't seem to be the case. Everything's spinning and I've thrown up twice and I still don't feel any better. But I don't think all of that is the alcohol. I'm not stupid.

That's my best friend (she's my *best friend*) in there, and I'm out here.

I watch her parents rush in and touch her and hug her and her mom is crying and they look like normal perfect parents, all blond hair and blue eyes and not at all who you'd expect would try to rehabilitate their gay son. The pajamas help the picture. If they were dressed, wrapped up in pashminas or some shit, they'd be too pretty to be real and you'd *know* there was something underneath, but no, they're wearing flannel pants with holes in them because they're *poor* and they look so plainspoken but they're not, they let Bianca get here when she should so goddamn be in inpatient and they focused on freaking *fine* James instead.

I'm looking down, and I watch his shoes come toward me, then hear his voice. "You all right?" He sounds like he's acting, like it's not really him.

I nod without raising my head.

"What the hell happened?"

"I picked her up and she was drunk. I took her over to Rachel's. We made her up. She wanted to go out. We went out. We had a fight, she went to the bathroom, Rachel found her collapsed in there, we brought her here, her blood pressure was too low, they gave her electrolytes and now she's okay. Her blood alcohol isn't even that high. They're bringing in a counselor to talk to her. Maybe a social worker. They weren't sure." I say it flat, like this is public-speaking class and I'm going to fail this speech.

"Why did you take her out?"

"She wanted to."

"She's fourteen, you should have told her no. What were you thinking?"

"She's my *friend*. I shouldn't have to be her mom, too." I don't know if I really have these feelings in me or if they've just sounded all night like something I should logically have, but now these words are coming out of me and they feel so true that they scare me.

And James is here, being the other half of me. "I don't care if you shouldn't have to do it, you told me that you had her tonight—"

But no. No. I can't fucking talk myself into this anymore. I can't freaking *talk to myself* anymore. I need to hash this out. I need to yell at somebody besides my *own damn self*. "She's old enough to make her own fucking decisions! And she wanted to go out and she wants to starve herself to death so who the hell am I to get in the way of that, how the hell much power do you think I have?" I'm on my feet now, and he grabs me by the wrist and pulls me outside. "Why does anyone think I'm a good influence? I stopped eating and I gave up on my friends just because they were mad at me and I'm still in love with my ex-girlfriend and I slut around to try to get rid of that and I'm using your best friend and here I am with your sister in the ER and you know what? If taking care of her is my responsibility, if I have to stand here and listen to your codependent bullshit, then maybe *you should have been the one doing this* instead of yelling at me because I didn't pick up the slack well enough!"

"Goddamn it, Etta."

"You've been doing this for *years*, I've been her friend for three months, and you expect me to come in here so you can take a fucking break—"

"*Yes*, okay? I want a fucking break! My baby sister's killing herself and there's nothing I can do and my parents are telling me there's something wrong with me and my boyfriend lives an hour away and *yes*, okay, *yes*, I want a *fucking break*."

"Well I'm not *you*, okay? I can't just be *assistant you* just because she wants me to be—"

"Why not? *Why the hell not?* That's what you do, isn't it?"

I'm cold. "What are you talking about?"

"You hitch yourself to somebody else and chase after that same goddamn dream, right? Being a lesbian? Going to Brentwood? Yeah, taking care of Bianca? Are the only two original things you've ever done starving yourself and going home with a guy from a club?"

"*Fuck you!*"

"God*damn it*, Etta, fight *back*! Stick up for yourself! What the hell good is that spark if you've got nothing to do with it?"

"I don't *know!*"

I don't *know*.

I start walking away and I don't even know where I'm going.

"Etta!" he shouts.

No. No.

Everything's blurry at the bus stop, and then a hand closes around my arm. I jump.

It's just Rachel. "Etta. C'mon, sweetie."

"Where are we going?" I'm already walking beside her.

"I'm gonna take you home."

"Okay . . ."

I shouldn't do this. I should go back. I should be with Bianca. I should be with James.

She pulls the seat belt over me and tucks a few loose dreads behind my ear. "Okay. Okay."

"I'm so tired . . ."

"Rest, baby girl."

I rest my head against the window. It's raining. When did it start raining? Was it raining when I was with James? Why don't I remember.

Drunk, still.

"Did you hate me?" I say.

"Etta. I never hated you. The Dykes got all caught up in this thing and I was sick, and then I was so busy with AP Chem, I didn't even see it. . . ."

Lying. She's lying.

She knew what was going on.

I just want her to be good or bad and this is so *frustrating*.

"We're not going to go to New York, are we," I say.

"That was just pretend."

It was just pretend.

It was all just pretend, maybe.

"Did you hate me?" When did I start crying? Maybe it's not raining.

"What are you talking about?"

"When I wasn't eating. Did you hate me?" I can't catch my breath. "You stopped talking to me, you didn't even, you didn't *know* I was getting better, is that why, was it too much, how could I have done that to you, and with Ben, why do I hurt you . . ."

The car isn't moving anymore, and I'm pulled into her.

"I could never, ever hate you," she says. "You're my whole world."

The thing is, that's *terrifying*.

I say, "You should hate me. You should fucking hate me," and it's true, and it's not true, and I know them both as much as I know that I am going to go home and shove my fingers down my throat.

22

FOR A WEEK I DON'T TALK TO ANYONE.

I tell my mom I have the flu, and throw up without hiding it a few times for good measure. *My stomach's too queasy to hold things down, Mom,* which doesn't exactly explain why after she and Kristina are asleep I sneak downstairs and eat all the ice cream and five bags of chips and the whole box of chocolates Mom's ex-boyfriend got her that she never threw away. I throw up in trash bags in my room because I know these tricks by now, and I can't keep myself from thinking *I bet Bianca doesn't binge, I bet Bianca isn't eating anything at all right now* and that leads right into *Bianca doesn't want you* and that leads into *you chickenshit piece of crap, she might still be in the hospital and you haven't called her.*

She doesn't call. Neither does James. Mason does, a few

times, but I don't answer. Ian calls too, once. For some reason I feel the most bad about avoiding him. The thought that he's innocent implies that the rest of them aren't, and that's messed up. I've already made them feel guilty for everything that's wrong with me. I should stop now.

I know I've gained weight. I don't think my toe shoes would even support me.

The details are so boring. The actual time it takes is so boring. I don't do anything new. I don't do anything I haven't done before. There is everything that was wrong with me swirled at the bottom of the toilet bowl. There is my exhaustion from it all. Here's the hunger and ache and damn *sadness* of it not being fun anymore.

It's so stupid, what pulls me, suddenly, out of it.

If I keep throwing up, I'm going to ruin my voice.

I didn't think I cared, so it doesn't make sense that I do.

It's only been a few days. I pull myself up. I eat normally and it's awful, but it's really surprising what you can learn to live with.

My little sister—my little sister who *dressed up as me for Halloween*—slips "Get Well" cards under my door.

When I was her age, I was worse than I am now. And here's Kristina being my role model, laughing at me in her bathrobe after I sneak a boy out, giving a shit when people don't like her.

Of course I'll try again for you, Kristina.

Of course.

• • •

My first day back at school after I decide to be a human again, Rachel's out "sick" again. I call her at lunch to make sure she's all right, and she is, but she sounds pissed at me for not returning her calls for a week and I can't exactly blame her, but at the same time it feels really far away from me. Everything does. Maybe I'm not doing so well at being a human, really.

I want to eat but I can't bring myself to do it in front of everyone, so I buy lunch at the cafeteria—salad, half sandwich, apple, water, cookie—and shove it into my school bag and head outside. The Dykes are out there holding unlit cigarettes, leaning against some boy's car because it's okay when they do it. Unless they all took up smoking in the last three months, they're all just holding them as props.

"Where you goin', Etta?" Isabel calls after me. Not friendly. "Don't you want to come hang out with us some more?" I guess the truce was only in play when they were drunk and Rachel was around.

I keep walking.

"Getting a little big for that skirt, Etta, aren't you?"

Natasha.

I turn around. She's pretending to blow a smoke ring with that cigarette that *isn't even lit*.

How was I ever scared of these girls?

These girls are *so small*.

"I don't know," I say. "But I'm getting too big for you."

She kicks me in the back and I scrape my palms up.

It's Wednesday afternoon, and Mom's at work and Kristina's at flute practice and I'm home alone because I skipped chorus and group and just came straight home like a loser. Last semester I would have been at Pride Alliance right now and that usually eats at me. Rachel was right. When you start dating guys, you don't just lose girls. You lose a whole sector of your life. If I end up marrying a guy, what the hell queer community is ever going to want me?

And there's just no answer to that. There isn't going to be some happy surprise ending. Rainbow kids are going to yell "breeder" at me when I'm out with a boy and they're never going to know I've done all the shit that they have. They're not going to know that I know what it's like to be gay in goddamn Nebraska.

I should just go back to dating girls. There's like fifteen lesbians in Nebraska and they were all at Cupcake that night and I'll just pick one, whatever.

But in the middle of feeling all sorry for myself, there's a knock on the door. And I can ignore a dozen phone calls but apparently I can't ignore this.

I open the door, and there she is, all seventy-eight (they

weighed her at the hospital. I didn't want to know) pounds of her. She gives me this smile I've never seen on her. It's warm. It's like Rachel, in such a good way.

I'm still in my damn uniform, I realize. Pleated skirt biting me in the waistband, white button-down, tie.

"Come on, Etta," she says. "Let's go for a ride."

23

IT'S ALL OF THEM. MASON DRIVING, JAMES IN THE PASSENGER seat, Ian and Bianca back here with me. Bianca looks a little better, maybe, definitely better than the last time I saw her. Ian gives my leg a rub over my kneesocks and Bianca, after a few miles, leans her head on my shoulder.

I guess on some level I thought they were taking me out to kill me and bury me in the woods.

"You're not mad?" I say.

Bianca kisses my shoulder. "We love you."

It's enough. Finally, it's enough.

"So I'm dropping out," James says. We're leaning against the pickup, watching Ian and Mason do rounds on the motorcycle. Bianca's maybe twenty feet away from us, turning slow circles with her arms in the air, tracing her toe on the soft ground.

"Of school?" Jealous.

He shakes his head. "The auditions."

"What? No."

He nods. "It's not right for me. I'm happy to stay here."

"No you're not." This is wrong.

He laughs a little. "Not everyone hates Nebraska."

This feels like completely new information.

"She really wants to stay," I realize.

"Yeah. She likes it here. She likes the weather. She likes knowing everybody. I'm thinking when I turn eighteen next month maybe I'll get us our own place."

"You can't stay for her," I say.

He laughs. It sounds more real this time. "Of course I can."

God, I feel like an idiot.

Of course he can. Of *course* he can. If I don't have any damn qualms about leaving my mom and my sister, how can I blame him for feeling the opposite? We need each other, James and I. We need these two sides of the same person. We need people who stay and people who go and this whole time I've been loving him and butting heads with him and trying to understand him and this whole time I couldn't figure out that he's the same as me, he is the exact damn opposite of me. Soul mates.

I spread my hand out like his.

"Besides," he says. "It's not just for her." He's watching the motorcycle. "For Mason. For . . . yeah, for Ian." He's blushing now, ducking his head. James. "We only have a year left before we're off who-knows-where. I want to have a nice last year and for me that means here."

"I thought you wanted a break from her sometimes?"

He laughs. "Then I'll go see a movie. And I'd miss her before it's over, probably."

I say, "You know, odds are I'm going to be stuck here, same as you."

"Nah. Even if you don't get in you won't be here." He tugs on my skirt playfully. "You're always going to be somewhere else."

"I'm one of the ones who's going."

"Yeah, like Mason. Though I'm guessing not together."

"I guess not." It's okay. "Listen . . . what you said at the hospital."

"Makes me a jackass."

"Yeah, but not an incorrect jackass."

He lights a cigarette and watches me.

I steal it and take a drag. "I've been thinking about it. What choices I made that were really mine. What it is that I'm actually wanting, here. Beyond this, you know. This vague thing about leaving."

"Wait, Etta, I can't remember, tell me again if you want to get out of Nebraska?"

I shove him. "It's more than that, though. That's not what I've been . . . well, dying for, I guess."

"All right, punch line, hit me."

"I'm thinking mainly I'm going to use this Brentwood audition as a free trip to New York. And once I'm there . . . I'm going to be there to look at ballet schools."

He smiles at me. "Yeah?"

"You know my whole life this was what I wanted. Prima ballerina."

"And you gave it up for Rachel."

I shake my head. "It's not that simple. I gave it up because I . . . didn't fit."

"Don't tell me you're talking about starving yourself again, because I'm kind of up to my ears in that." He kisses my cheek.

"No, I just . . . I can be chubby and still be poised, you know? I was stupid for thinking it's one or the other." I can rein my Etta-ness in while I'm onstage. I can do that. If ballet wants that, I'll give it that.

It's my best friend. If it wants me to give something up, I will.

That's how this works with me.

Something Bianca told me once is clawing at the back of my brain, though, but I can't remember what it was, so calm down, brain. Everything's fine.

I say, "So that's it, I guess. I'll see if there's somewhere I can abscond to next year, somewhere my mom might sign off on, or I'll talk to people at colleges if that's all she'll let me do."

"Sounds like a plan."

"You'll really be okay here?"

"Yeah," he says. "I like Nebraska." He smiles out at Bianca. "I like the weather."

I meet Mason and Ian when they get off the motorcycle. Mason watches me while he fiddles with the strap of his helmet. He can't figure out if he's keeping it on or taking it off.

I don't know what to say to him, just because I feel like everything has already been said. I didn't answer his calls. He stopped calling. There isn't anything complicated about this. There never was.

The only thing that maybe makes it harder is that I really, truly liked him, and I hope he liked me too.

I really think he did.

Does.

He stops playing with the strap on his helmet. He keeps it on. "This was fun," he said.

I'm smiling. "Yeah. It was really fun."

He holds out the other helmet. "Want to go for a ride?"

Yeah. I do.

"Are you gonna buy me something?" Bianca asks. She's balancing, toe-heel, toe-heel on the dirty ridge that separates the road from the cornfield. The corn is green now, starting to grow.

"Like what?"

"Like when my aunt went to France she brought me an Eiffel Tower snow globe."

"I don't think they'll have any of those."

She shoves me and loses her balance, wavers a little.

"You okay?" I ask.

"Uh-huh." She keeps going. We haven't talked about what happened at the club, and I keep thinking we're going to, and then I realize there really isn't anything to say. We did all these things and felt all these things and those things exist and we are still okay. It was like cutting open a blister, and the thing is that this happened and we're still okay.

It's so weird, to really be friends with someone.

"C'mere." I pull her up onto my back and we walk a little ways like this. This is such a stupid thing to think, and there's no way I'm saying it out loud, but she's a little heavier than I would have expected. Maybe this is the first time I've thought of her as an actual person with the weight of bones and organs and blood. When I carried her out of Cupcake she didn't weigh anything.

"Do you think you'll get in?" she says.

"Nah." I don't tell her about ballet schools right now. I don't need to.

"What if you do? Will you go?"

"Do you think I should?"

"Uh-huh."

"You don't want me around anymore?"

She kicks at my hands with the toes of her shoes. "You'll still come home. Your family lives here."

"I'd visit you."

"Who says I'll be here?"

I'm cold, suddenly. I put her down. Gently.

"What does that mean?" I say.

She looks at the sky all fake-casual, like there's something up there she's more interested in than me. She squints some. I almost believe it.

She says, "I've been talking about inpatient?" like it's a question. (Like this should have ever been a question.)

"Yeah?" I try not to sound too eager. "Talking with who?"

She laughs. "Guess."

"James?"

"No. He'd try to talk me out of it."

It's sick that I believe that. Not sick. Just sad. That I know that however messed up Bianca is, James still thinks that just loving her enough will fix it, that there's no way they could be better apart, just for a little, than they would be together. I don't think he's wrong not to try for the audition. The chances he'd get in are tiny, anyway. He's not as good as she is. And he doesn't want her to think that there's even the smallest chance he would leave.

I say, "Okay, then who."

"Angela."

"Shut up, really?"

"You stopped coming to group, what else was I going to do!"

For some reason I'm really baffled that she kept going to group even when I didn't. I think a part of me still thinks that Bianca is a windup toy someone needs to crank. Maybe she is, more than she should be. But we've all got our faults, so I should stop trying to make a poem or a statement or a damn thesis out of hers.

"She thinks it would be a good idea," Bianca says. "Everyone at the hospital was saying it too. I didn't think I'd really reached . . . that point. Any point."

"You okay?"

She shrugs. "I want to keep going."

"I know, baby."

"I didn't get there."

"To where?"

She shrugs again. "Seventy. Sixty. I don't know. Ten."

"Hit ninety before I'm back from the audition and I'll give you a snow globe." When weight gain happens in eating disorders, it happens fast.

"Two snow globes."

"Brat."

She smiles, just for a second, then says, "I don't know, Etta."

"Where's our miracle cure, right?"

"I want to get better!" she shouts, up at the sky, and then she looks at me and says, "Why doesn't that just *work*?"

"I love you, Bee."

"Love you."

"If I figure it out, I'll tell you."

"Promise?"

"Promise."

We link pinkies back to the car.

The funny thing is that the Dykes would approve of this.

The funnier thing is that I don't give a shit.

I just like her.

24

MY MOM DRIVES ME TO THE AIRPORT. MY BRAIN HAS STOPPED going *NewYorkNewYorkNewYork* for long enough for me to remember to be scared out of my mind. I know I'm meeting up with a group when I get there, but I have no idea if any of them are on the same plane as me or how many of us there are. Five got through from my region. Four now, without James. I really wish he had gone through with this and just thrown the audition or something, just so I wouldn't be alone. Codependent pot calling the codependent kettle codependent, yeah, I know.

My mom gives me a hundred dollars "for emergencies" and hugs me before security and says, "Ugh, sweetie. Kick ass."

She looks tired. She's keeping her sunglasses on now that we're outside so that people won't see her dark circles because she cares what all these people will think of her. But she didn't hide them from me in the car.

I think about Bianca's parents in their pajamas and my mom here in her sharp business suit, her straight edges, and she overflows for me, you know?

She tries so hard.

She loves me so much.

I hug her tight.

I take Benadryl and sleep on the plane, which is lovely except for the part where I'm still kind of stupid when I get off. It takes me a while of wandering around with my bag before I find my group, and once I do I don't know how I missed them. There are these three geeky-looking adults with signs that say BRENTWOOD AUDITIONS and some teenagers crowded around them. Here's the part I can't believe: there's like fifty of them. At most.

Either the other regions sucked or mine encompassed more area than I thought. But . . . holy shit. I actually have a shot at this.

I could be going to a *musical theater* school.

And I'm trying to keep my focus, *I'm here for ballet, these guys are suckers for bringing me here because I'm here for ballet ballet ballet* but I blink and see myself and *Into the Woods* and *Cabaret* and *Guys and Dolls* and *A Chorus Line*, the show that maybe I'll never see.

And then a few more people show up and we walk outside and get into a bus and New York hits me like a pile of dirty beautiful bricks.

I'm not saying it's original or exciting. But I'm also not going to pretend like the past few months and my kinds of startling ties to a handful of these damn Nebraskans have changed how I feel. I don't know how I ever expected to fall in love with Mason, with anybody, when here was this city waiting for me.

I could go on forever. I could talk about Chelsea that changes personalities at every street or the Midtown that everyone pictures and how hushed you feel going over the Brooklyn Bridge. I could write these long emails home about *no, Mom, the Statue of Liberty is on an island but look at this pizza place, look at this restaurant of just peanut butter, look at the parts of the city that really do sleep.*

But then they take us through those doors and I see that BRENTWOOD marquee and there are people, these normal-looking people, laughing and wearing not-uniforms and yelling across the halls of the dorms, and I hear *The Phantom of the Opera* playing from somewhere in here, and oh my God I'm not in New York, not anymore.

I'm at the damn Brentwood School.

And something in me just changed.

I think most people in our group are trying to pretend this isn't cool, or maybe they're just genuinely not freaking out as much as I am, but I make friends with these two kids, Skyler and Stephanie, and we stand in the back of the group during our tour and dig our nails into each other's hands because holy shit did you see the size of that rehearsal room and oh my God is that a bell tower and how does everyone look so *happy*?

And then we see the girl crying in the bathroom that they try to usher us past and I'm thinking, *aha, seeing through the cracks, these people are secretly miserable, this is a manufactured tour*, and then another girl goes into the bathroom and holds her and three more come in a minute later and join them and oh God I want to be here, I want to curl up in that bathroom and go to sleep.

"We'll be calling you in alphabetically to meet with the board starting at ten tomorrow," the geekiest clipboarder says, passing out schedules. "Please don't be late. In the meantime your room assignments are here, and you're expected to be in your room by—"

Yeah, who cares—we're *staying in the dorms*. I take all these pictures on my phone of every damn corner of the room and of Stephanie and Skyler geeking the hell out, even though I have no idea who I'm going to send them to. I don't want to make Bianca jealous when she's been so amazing. Kristina wouldn't understand. Rachel would . . . I don't know. I guess I need to deal with her at some point, but Nebraska seems far away, and that isn't because I'm in New York, because right now I really couldn't give less of a shit about the (yeah, crappy) view outside my dorm window, because right now I'm sitting on my bed talking to a boy who says he's bisexual and "Oh, yeah, everyone here is great about it, the queer groups make sure to be so inclusive," and I am trying not to cry.

I need this.

God, I forgot for a minute that I'm here to look at ballet schools.

And then I remember something else.

I'm not good enough for Brentwood.

I'm here to look at ballet schools.

Stephanie's my roommate and we stay up late. She's singing "For Good" from *Wicked* and her voice reminds me of Bianca's, deep, alto, but she's . . . in all honesty, she's better than Bianca. Maybe in a few years Bianca will be there. Stephanie's seventeen like me, after all. And she's got broad shoulders, a chest, something to support that voice.

She wants me to sing for her but I'm so scared of waking people up, of waking people up with my goddamn mediocre voice, that I just end up sitting on the floor against my bed with my iPod listening to "At the Ballet" over and over again.

Maggie hits that high note and I push my face into my knees.

25

THE AUDITION SCHEDULE IS POSTED AND MINE ISN'T UNTIL THE afternoon, so I look up the addresses—hooray, so many years of fantasy-walking the streets of New York, I know exactly where they are—for a bunch of ballet schools and I do a few jumping jacks to amp myself up because it is go-time, Etta "Kick It in the Ass" Sinclair, let's do this. Ballet or bust.

I choose one sort of because it's nearby but mostly because it's near what sounds like a really good Indian restaurant in the village and I guess that's the place I'm in with food right now and hell if I'm going to question it. I call and they say someone can give me an unofficial tour, and then I eat first, because I'm afraid two hundred ballerinas will scare me right out of that good place I'm in, and where I sit outside I can see some girls walking down the sidewalk with duffels and leg warmers, some leaning against the front of the building and smoking cigarettes, some laughing and hanging out in the courtyard behind the building. They're tiny and white, big surprise, and they all have that flat stiff-necked way of walking, but they're talking to each other, laughing, gesturing in that effortlessly beautiful way only dancers can and I never know if I do too, with those wrists and those fingers like you don't care, like everything's rehearsed and learned and memorized.

I go to the front desk and sign something and eventually this student comes out who seems bored but nice and takes me on a tour. "This is our practice studio," she says. "This is our cafeteria, and this is . . . our other practice studio." She giggles. "And here's another practice studio . . ."

We finally go into a practice studio that actually has people practicing. A choreographer is ordering around a bunch of them, but most of the rest are in small groups—"wait, I thought it was stage right first," "wait, I thought *frappe* was first"—and a few younger girls are stretching in the corner, maybe about to take their place, plié-ing and *revelé*-ing and making me miss being a kid.

I stretch out one leg and point my toe, just a little. I'm wearing leggings and I have my pointe shoes in my bag, just in case, but right now it's enough just to stretch out a little with the kids, to be part of something.

My tour guide goes over to the choreographer, and he laughs at something she says and takes a swig from a water bottle. He asks her a question, she smiles and points to me, and then he's motioning at me to come over.

"How many years?" he says. It's a pretty common opener.

I was this little fat-legged kid running all the way up the stairs to her first class while my mom panted and paused on the second flight, yelling at me to wait up. "Thirteen years."

"On pointe for how long?"

"Five years."

"And you're how old?"

"Seventeen."

He smiles. "Impressive."

"*Merci.*"

"And you're interested in the school?"

"Uh-huh." I don't need to mention that I have no idea under what circumstances I could end up here. I don't know if I'm really interested in the school or if I'm just interested in saying good-bye to Nebraska.

He slings his bag over his shoulder and says, "I'm off for a period. Of course I can't officially . . ."

"No, of course."

"Can't officially *anything*, but I would like to see you dance, if you don't mind?"

I'm not an idiot. I know why he wants to see me dance, and I know it's because I don't look even a little like any of the girls in this room, and hey, if it gets me a look and it gets him to see me I'll take it, right? He wants to know how I dance with this body, and maybe he wants to know if I'm the black girl I bet they'd like to have at this school, and I will pretty gladly be his experiment if it means I get to dance for someone who knows ballet for the first time in what feels like a billion years.

But then he takes me to this small practice room and I lace up my shoes and holy shit, I'm scared to death.

"Any routine you know," he says. "No pressure. Whatever you're comfortable with."

What I'm comfortable with.

Rachel's lap.

Sticking my fingers down my throat.

Geometry proofs.

My attic.

Bianca.

Bianca.

Bianca in my attic.

Fouettés.

I dance.

It feels good. I know I'm doing well, and he's smiling, and I just go and go and go and I'm this free animal, I'm this little bird with a big ass and I am nailing these moves and I am doing them free and big and *me*, I am sinking into them and spinning out of them and I'm stretched and long and beautiful. I'm not wearing the right clothes for this and I don't care. I haven't practiced being up on pointe again enough and I don't care. I don't care about anything because I am in New York and I am dancing at a ballet school and this, this is the dream, this was always the dream.

Except I stop, and that's it.

The magic's gone.

It was only here when I was moving.

He smiles and says, "You're a fantastic dancer."

"Thank you."

There's a *but*.

He thinks a long time before he says, "But—and by no means is this the final word, and you should absolutely audition—"

"Right."

"I think you should think hard about if this is the right place for you."

I don't fit.

He says, "There's not a thing wrong with you, my dear, but you don't perform ballet like a ballerina. There's a certain kind of poise, of control—"

Control.

"—a kind of discipline—"

Discipline.

"That I'm not sure I see in you. You're a lovely ballet dancer, Etta. But I'm not sure right now that you're a ballerina. But like I said, I'm far from the final word, and we're not looking for perfect dancers. Just dancers who look like they want to be taught."

"I don't look like I want to be taught?"

He laughs, not altogether warmly this time. "You look like you're already doing it how you want to be doing it."

"Oh."

He says, "No, I just . . . There's a looseness about you, Etta. There's a bit of unpredictability in the way you move. It isn't bad, but it isn't something that's likely to make you a solid part of a company. You have to be able to hold certain positions stiffly, to execute moves with complete precision, and you seem to favor something a bit . . ."

More free.

I favor something a bit more free.

"Thank you," I say. "Thank you for seeing me."

I'm walking back to Brentwood, and I just finally put the fucking pieces together.

Rachel was wrong. I was wrong. Ballet was not the problem.

This, dancing, me, was never the problem.

It was these damn programs.

It was these damn rules.

It was everything that wasn't *my feet, the music, me*.

It was all this stuff shoving me into a box that is too small.

It was all the shit I just do not need in my life anymore.

Back at Brentwood, I turn wild pirouettes that throw me into the trash cans in the hallways and people laugh and laugh and cheer me on. I am curves instead of lines, but that is still shapes. That is still dancing. I'm not wrong, and neither was the school, we just weren't right for each other, but beautiful ballet can still be right for me.

I don't know where all this perspective is coming from except from the part of me that really wants to logically justify how goddamn much I want to go to Brentwood, holy shit.

Who cares that they don't have a good dance department.

I would be their dance department. I would be the fucking crap out of it.

I'm sitting outside the audition room between John Sable and Mila Tran. They're not exactly chatty, but I can't blame them because fuck if I am either. Every once in a while a real student walks by and wishes us luck and toggles their feet between our sneakers or whatever, like foot-flirting, and then they're gone and I might as well not be in Brentwood, goddamn lovely Brentwood, anymore, because this is just any audition which means I'm just scared out of my mind.

It's not in an auditorium, which on one hand is good because holy shit don't put me on a stage right now, please, but it's also freaking scary because it's just in this classroom and I don't know what it looks like in there. I know we don't get a piano. I know that I can hear just the blur of everyone's voices in there and every single one of them sounds really good.

This isn't like the first round and maybe even the second round where I could scrape by on being just okay. Being funny isn't going to get me anywhere here. They don't care about my personality, they care about my talent. And I don't have enough.

scared shitless I text Bianca as John Sable goes in.

She responds almost immediately. She's still at home. She has her inpatient check-in later today. I won't be there.

just remember she says. *beeeee yourself*

Fucking *Aladdin* quote. This shouldn't make me feel better. But it does.

Because you know what, screw it. I'm the girl who's inspired by people telling her the damn cliché to be herself. I'm the girl who's too loud and too much and too *big* for a lot of people. I'm the girl who got through two rounds of cutthroat auditions on her damn personality.

So what the hell, right? Let's see this shit through.

I text just *bee* back, and then Sable comes out and it's my turn.

There's a whole group of people in the front, and I know it's the board, and I don't know why I was expecting a bunch of white guys in suits, I mean, this is musical theater. They're half girls, a quarter minorities, which is obviously better than Nebraska so I'll take it, and they're definitely at least a third gay so that should be cool, but somehow that makes this all a hundred times scarier because eesh, these aren't just clipboarded people I don't know, these are grown-up versions of me, these are people who I actually want to like me.

Okay. All right.

"Say your name and age, please?" one of them says. A black woman. Of course. Deep breath. "Etta Sinclair. Seventeen."

"What are you singing for us, Etta?"

"'At the Ballet.' Sheila's part."

She smiles a little and sits back. "Whenever you're ready."

I start immediately because I know I'm never going to be ready. The first part is talky. I'll ease myself into it. I barely have to do anything. It's just brassy Sheila. Okay. I start.

And—

Oh shit.

This is Maggie's part.

Motherfuck.

They're staring at me like I'm confused. I'm this close to apologizing, starting over, but then I'm just still talking, oh God, I'm still going.

> Anyway, I did have a fantastic fantasy life. I used
> to dance around the living room with my arms
> up like this

I don't do the ballerina pose. I saw Kay Cole on YouTube just hold her arms out like she's ready to catch someone. She didn't look like a dancer. She looked like a girl.

I do that.

I get through her monologue, and now, presumably,

they're going to want me to actually sing, but Maggie's singing part doesn't come immediately after, so I kind of fake my way through the next section, working myself through three-part harmonies and they're smiling at me, not mean, and I guess this is the part where I show off that goofy damn personality of mine except it's an *accident*, but whatever, I try to smile but if I keep looking I'm going to crack and laugh and not try so I close my eyes and then I have to do it. I can't back out now.

Everything was beautiful at the ballet
Raise your arms, and someone's always there

Oh yes, Etta, cry. That will help your voice.

I take a pause that's a little too long because this is it. This is the moment, and here I am and I didn't know that I wanted to be here, I had no damn clue, and here I am. Singing this part I've never been able to sing. Being this vulnerable dreamy girl instead of that brassy jaded dancer and here I am. Here I just . . . am.

I'm Etta Sinclair and I am a ballerina.

Yes, everything was beautiful at the ballet

This is where Sheila and Bebe slide up gently to a higher note. Maggie doesn't do that. Maggie climbs higher.

At the ballet!

That part went okay. That was okay.

She just shouts it out, is the thing. She's not singing, really, she's . . . exclaiming. It's not pretty and vibratoed. Maggie isn't trying to be pretty. She's just trying to feel something.

So. What the hell, right?

At the ballet!

Holy shit.

I hit it.

I hit it and I just *stick there*, because nope I flat-out refuse to break this off now, I am the girl who aces tests because I *decide I will, damnit,* and I hold it long and hard and I shake with it and then I finally drop off and I just stand there and I'm just ragged with the Maggie-ness, I'm standing there panting and crying and God, this is so embarrassing, a real singer could do that in her sleep.

They don't clap. It's okay. I don't think that's what this is.

"Sheila, huh?" the black woman says, with this side-leaning smile.

"Heh. Didn't work out how I planned."

"Why don't you tell us why you think Brentwood would be a good place for you?"

I should have prepared something. Shit. Who the hell would be surprised by this question?

But the thing is, I know why I think I belong here.

Because of one little girl.

I say, "I have this friend . . . my best friend. She's really into God. I don't know if I . . . but anyway, she told me this story and it's about this really religious guy like on his deathbed, uh, let's call him Bob, and he's *so* scared, and everyone who loves him is like . . . 'why are you scared? You've lived this fucking perfect life—sorry—and you are like as close to Moses and Jesus and stuff as anyone ever asked,' and he's like . . . 'I'm not scared God's going to ask me why wasn't I more like Moses and Jesus, he's going to ask me why wasn't I more Bob-ish. Why wasn't I as Bob-ish as I could possibly be?' And I'm like . . . not saying that I'm anything like Moses or Jesus because I curse and drink and sleep with girls, and I don't even think I believe in God or anything, but I think that if I went here and I tried to sing and I didn't back down and I met people who think being different is okay and who let me do ballet in the halls and stuff, and I listened and I grew up, then I wouldn't ever have to worry that I'm shrinking . . . sh-shrinking myself down, and no one could ever think that I . . . I think that I could be the most Etta-ish I could be. And I think that would be really good."

I think I'd be finally running *to* something instead of just *away*.

I wouldn't be trying to disappear.

She nods and writes this all down like I said something rational and clear and then says, "Do you want to tell us a little about yourself, Etta?"

"I . . . okay. Yeah. Of course."

I don't know a little about me. I don't think there's any sort of "little" of me. I don't know how to tell them that. I don't know how much I can take with me and bring with me. I don't know how much of this I want to keep. I don't know what's going to happen to Bianca, or if Rachel and I are going to be friends again. I don't even know what I'm going to do when I have to go back to Nebraska now that I know that this is here, that I could have had it, if maybe I'd sung the right part or been a different person.

So I just say it. The only thing I know for sure is true about me at this point, because this is the thing I want to say *"fuck you"* to everyone about. That's how I know. I'm so going to hell.

"I'm Etta Sinclair. And I'm a ballerina."

The list is posted on the bulletin board by the audition room at eight p.m. I heard a rumor they were admitting four people. But there are only three.

Garrett Meyers
Stephanie Brown
Me.

26

I CAN'T TALK TO ANYONE BECAUSE I CAN'T BREATHE, SO THE celebration comes in this blur of hugs from Stephanie, shattered people standing around me who didn't get in, oh God, and a flurry of text messages to my mom, Kristina, Bianca, James, Mason, Ian. After a lot of hemming and hawing that I decide is way too much hemming and hawing, someone else, one last person.

Everyone's congratulating me, everyone's so proud — Mason says he always knew I could do it, James says he knew it from the first second he met me, Mom says *oh my God baby I am SO PROUD, YES YOU CAN GO*, and Ian gives me just *congratulations!!* because he only knows me through James and the leg of my school skirt, it's fine.

But I don't hear from Kristina or Bianca, and that scares the shit out of me.

Fifteen minutes later my phone finally buzzes with a new message. It's from Bianca, and it's just a picture of her on a big medical scale. Her face is all red and swollen around her nose and eyes, baby, but she's smiling in the picture anyway, giving the finger to the camera that's pointed at an angle so I can see ninety-three on her scale.

Fuck yes, Bianca. YES.

I put my phone back into my pocket and my fingers brush that emergency hundred-dollar bill and yep, in that moment it's settled.

Before we go to the airport, me and Stephanie and this girl Lena who wants souvenirs (who says she's happy for me with this look on her face like she totally isn't, but I don't really blame her for it) duck into a couple of bodegas and they buy their I ♥ NY shirts and their MANHATTAN MANHATTAN MANHATTAN bags and let's not even pretend that I wouldn't love one, getting in hasn't suddenly made me classy, but I'm here for something else, and it doesn't take me long before I find a place selling ugly, absolutely tiny plastic snow globes with the Statue of Liberty or the Empire State Building or mini Times Squares in them.

Eighty-five cents each.

"How many of these do you have?"

And with the extra money I buy a fucking hot dog from a stand and I eat every last bite.

• • •

Rachel picks me up from the airport. While I was gone, spring break started. She went to Cabo for a few days and is tan and gorgeous now, like she wasn't already, but whatever.

I think she's pissed I didn't text her until the morning after, but I just forgot, it wasn't some big thing. (Or maybe the fact that I forgot is a big thing.)

"So are you going to go?" she says, and maybe it's weird that I never considered *not* going, but I really didn't. Jesus, it must have broken Bianca's heart to turn this down.

But for some reason I only say, "I think so." God, why am I still scared of this girl?

Or maybe I'm not scared. Maybe I just know she doesn't want me to go.

"I don't know," she says. "I mean, it's great that you got in, but isn't that a lot of pressure? And you'd be getting out of here in a year for college anyway."

"Rachel, what are you doing?"

She says, "I just think you should really think about whether this is the best thing for you. Dancing made you miserable, and it's not like you were ever really into musical theater except as something to watch, right?" She adjusts her grip on the steering wheel, staring straight ahead. "I mean, you never auditioned for that kind of thing here. Weren't you just trying out because Bianca was?"

The thing is that the way she says this, she's not devaluing why I auditioned, not really.

She's saying that doing that doesn't make sense now that she knows Bianca and I aren't a couple. She's devaluing Bianca.

The funny part is, it would have made perfect sense to her if I'd followed *her* somewhere.

"I'm going to go," I say. I don't say, *you're a good person, Rachel, but you don't want to be friends with me unless you can control me.* There's no point in saying it. I know it. And once I'm gone, she will too.

Still, I hope she comes and visits me sometimes. I'd like to get coffee with her.

"So how are the Dykes?" I say, and that's when I notice she's in flip-flops that show off her pedicure. Cropped, straight-leg jeans. Expensive sunglasses that are definitely not seventies.

"I don't know," she says. She shrugs a little. "They got boring."

"You're gonna be okay, Ray."

Bianca's in inpatient, James says. She started a few days ago. The picture she sent me was from her intake.

"I've visited her a few times," he says. "They've got her on a feeding tube, the kind down her nose, not in her stomach. Which I think is less serious or something. I guess that's a good sign."

We're sitting in my car, which is weird after so much time spent in his pickup truck. He looks too small here, crammed in.

"So when do you leave?" he says.

"Not for ages. August."

"Still have to finish out this school year, I guess."

"Unfortunately."

"We're going to miss you."

"Hey, don't. I'll be back for Thanksgiving and Christmas, you'll hardly know I was gone."

"You should get a New York accent so we don't forget."

"I'll work on that. Know what I'm doing this summer?"

"What?"

"Taking some goddamn singing lessons."

He laughs. "Fair enough."

"Will Bianca be out by then?"

"Oh, yeah, definitely. They're saying just a month probably, then intensive outpatient, half days and stuff, a meal. They keep saying it could have been a lot worse and like, great, that's exactly what she needs to hear."

"Ugh."

"But I've been looking at apartments for us. There are ones close to home, y'know, so it will feel less like we're running away, and that means close to the hospital too. They're pretty shitty, but I think she'll like fixing it up."

"I have decorations for you guys!"

"What?"

"Stuff I bought in New York."

"You should put them around her hospital room."

"They'll let me do that?"

"What? Yeah. It's not prison."

"I can visit her?"

"That thing I just said about it not being prison . . ."

I hug him and say, "Want to know something sick?"

"Only always."

"You guys almost made me want to stay here."

"Don't insult me like that."

"I love you, you know."

"You. You're our success story," he says.

"Yeah, well. You're mine."

He rests his head on my shoulder.

When I get to the treatment center, though, they tell me Bianca's sleeping. "She does a lot of that," one of the nurses says. "You can wake her up."

The stupid thing is that I used to dream of being somewhere like this. White walls and concerned doctors who understand what you're going through and mutter about how much weight you've lost and put tubes in you because they don't trust you to physically eat on your own. I read stories about girls in treatment and watched documentaries about how they'd smear their mashed potatoes in their hair whenever a nurse turned her head rather than eat them. They were these superheroes of tragedy. This was my goal.

I don't think Bianca's hiding her mashed potatoes anywhere. I think that at some point in this she probably will, and that sucks, but right now she's being so tough and I can't shake the feeling she's doing it for me.

It's the best thing that's ever happened to me, is the thing. Better than sex. Better than Brentwood.

"I don't need to wake her up," I say. "Just need to put some things up in her room."

The nurse nods and lets me in.

Bianca's face is kind of puffy because weight gain goes to your face first. She's curled up with her arms far away from her body, I think so she won't accidentally feel herself and the weight she's gained. I know that feeling. I might still sleep like that. I'm not sure.

I set my enormous paper bag on the floor and take out each snow globe, one by one, and find places to set and stack and balance them in her room. After the first forty or so it turns into a real challenge. I carefully pull her nightstand drawer open and arrange a bunch around her Bible. I trace some up her body like an outline, carefully not touching. I put four on her pillow. I put two in each of her slippers sitting by the door. They're knocking over and falling off all the time, but the nice thing about them being made out of cheap plastic is, they kind of just bounce. The other nice thing is that I could afford ninety-three of them.

Ninety-three snow globes for my ninety-three-pound girl.

I write *BE BEE* on her whiteboard before I go.

• • •

So I'm feeling pretty great about everything until I walk into my room and there's Kristina crying on my bed.

"Hey hey hey whoa. What's wrong?"

"Were you even going to tell me you were leaving?"

"I texted you. . . ."

"*Texted* me?"

"I know. Shit. Okay, c'mere." I sit on my bed and wrap my arms around her. "I haven't even seen you since I got home."

"You didn't look for me."

"Where were you?"

"Backyard. In our tree." When Kristina and I were little we had a tree we decided was a castle and we stole branches from other trees to make walls and really bad turrets. We made veils out of leaves and helmets out of sticks and we were warriors and princesses.

"Baby."

"You were just gonna leave?"

"Hey, I'm not leaving until August."

She sniffles and rests her head on my shoulder and says, "I never see you anymore," and God Christ she's right. I never see her anymore.

But this girl is *so important*. This girl loved me all the time that nobody else did while I moped around saying I had no friends. This girl let me date boys and girls and teased me and never judged me. This girl wants to be a librarian and to rest her head in my lap while I read her books. This girl is my little sister and I should not be teaching her that people who love her can ignore her. That is not okay.

This girl was me for Halloween and that should never, will never, stop being amazing.

I pull her up and hug her. "Want to go shopping? And you can tell me what's going on with school."

"Girls suck."

"Yep. Come on, shopping fixes everything."

It's so stupid.

She smiles.

"Yeah," I say. "Let's go shopping."

She buys earrings and a dress and a pair of sunglasses and I buy her a whole outfit in case she wants to dress up as me and not have "BITCH" across her tits. And I buy a whole bunch of shit that fits my new body.

My phone buzzes and I take it out of my purse and holy shit, it's a reply to that last text I sent after I got in, the one that never got answered.

> so psyched you're going to be here. dinner & a
> shitty movie when you move in, ok? we've got
> talking to do —danielle

ACKNOWLEDGMENTS

Writing this book has been a long and unbelievable experience. I wrote my very first story about Etta when I was still in high school. The number of people who have helped me develop her and her world since then is truly uncountable, but here's the part where I do my best.

So I give infinite, enormous thank-yous to Leah Goodreau, who draws me beautiful pictures; to Seth Keating, my rock; and Abby, Kim, and Saul, my beautiful family. I know reading this one might not have been the easiest for you, and your support and bravery mean the world to me.

My agent, John Cusick, continues to be everything I need and more, and Liesa Abrams, Michael Strother, the immortal Bethany Buck, and the entire Pulse team sparkles with their enthusiasm and their indulgence of my wild stubbornness. A special shout-out to Karina Granda, the magician behind what might be my favorite of all of my book covers.

To the incredible writers who continue to support me every day: my Musers, always; my *Supernatural* sister, Courtney Summers; my work wife, Kody Keplinger; and so many more: thank you for being the reassurance that people with so much talent think that I'm worth their time.

To anyone who has ever dealt with any sort of eating disorder, thank you for making me want to write a book about us with your passion and your courage for sharing your stories, and please know that there is so much hope, and that I am always here for you if you want to reach out, to either offer whatever support I can or to refer you to someone much more competent.

And to some miscellaneous humans who fill up my world: my lovely aunts, uncles, cousins, and grandparents; Anica Rissi; Jeff Gasikowski; the good people who deliver food to my apartment; and some generally acceptable cats.

And to my gorgeous, incredible, perfect readers, who give me the ability to have food delivered to my apartment. You fucking incredible citizens of my heart.

Turn the page for a peek at
GONE, GONE, GONE.

"Written with depth and heart and a quirky sweetness that I just adore. These are characters I will never forget."
—AMY REED, author of *Beautiful* and *Clean*

GONE, GONE, GONE

HANNAH MOSKOWITZ
author of BREAK and INVINCIBLE SUMMER

Stonewall
Honor Book
American Library Association

CRAIG

I WAKE UP TO A QUIET WORLD.

There's this stillness so strong that I can feel it in the hairs on the backs of my arms, and I can right away tell that this quiet is the sound of a million things and fourteen bodies not here and one boy breathing alone.

I open my eyes.

I can't believe I slept.

I sit up and swing my feet to the floor. I'm wearing my shoes, and I'm staring at them like I don't recognize them, but they're the shoes I wear all the time, these black canvas high-tops from Target. My mom bought them for me. I have that kind of mom.

I can feel how cold the tile is. I can feel it through my shoes.

I make kissing noises with my mouth. Nothing answers. My brain is telling me, my brain has been telling me for every single second since I woke up, exactly what is different, but I am not going to think it, I won't think it, because they're all just hiding or upstairs. They're not gone. The only thing in the whole world I am looking at is my shoes, because everything else is exactly how it's supposed to be, because they're not gone.

But this, this is wrong. That I'm wearing shoes. That I slept in my shoes. I think it says something about you when you don't even untie your shoes to try to go to bed. I think it's a dead giveaway that you are a zombie. If there is a line between zombie and garden-variety insomniac, that line is a shoelace.

I got the word "zombie" from my brother Todd. He calls me "zombie," sometimes, when he comes home from work at three in the morning—Todd is so old, old enough to work night shifts and drink coffee without sugar—and comes down to the basement to check on me. He walks slowly, one hand on the banister, a page of the newspaper crinkling in his hand. He won't flick on the light, just in case I'm asleep, and there I am, I'm on the couch, a cat on each of my shoulders and a man with a small penis on the TV telling me how he became a man with a big penis, and I can too. "Zombie," Todd will say softly, a hand on top of my head. "Go to sleep."

Todd has this way of being affectionate that I see but usually don't feel.

I say, "Someday I might need this."

"The penis product?"

"Yes." Maybe not. I think my glory days are behind me. I am fifteen years old, and all I have is the vague hope that, someday, someone somewhere will once again care about my penis and whether it is big or small.

The cats don't care. Neither do my four dogs, my three rabbits, my guinea pig, or even the bird I call Flamingo because he stands on one leg when he drinks, even though that isn't his real name, which is Fernando.

They don't care. And even if they did, they're not here. I can't avoid that fact any longer.

I am the vaguest of vague hopes of a deflated heart.

I look around the basement, where I sleep now. My alarm goes off, even though I'm already up. The animals should be scuffling around now that they hear I'm awake, mewing, rubbing against my legs, and whining for food. This morning, the alarm is set for five thirty for school, and my bedroom is a silent, frozen meat locker because the animals are gone.

Here's what happened, my parents explain, weary over cups of coffee, cops come and gone, all while I was asleep.

What happened is that I slept.

I slept through a break-in and a break-out, but I couldn't sleep through the quiet afterward. This has to be a metaphor for something, but I can't think, it's too quiet.

Broken window, jimmied locks. They took the upstairs TV and parts of the stereo. They left all the doors open. The house is as cold as October. The animals are gone.

It was a freak accident. Freak things happen. I should be used to that by now. Freaks freaks freaks.

Todd was the one to come home and discover the damage. My parents slept through it too. This house is too big.

I say, "But the break-in must have been hours ago."

My mother nods a bit.

I say, "Why didn't I wake up as soon as the animals escaped?"

My mom doesn't understand what I'm talking about, but this isn't making sense to me. None of it is. Break-ins aren't supposed to happen to us. We live in a nice neighborhood in a nice suburb. They're supposed to happen to other people. I am supposed to be so tied to the happiness and the comfort of those animals that I can't sleep until every single one is fed, cleaned, hugged. Maybe if I find enough flaws in this, I can make it so it never happened.

This couldn't have happened.

At night, Sandwich and Carolina and Zebra sleep down at my feet. Flamingo goes quiet as soon as I put a sheet over his cage. Peggy snuggles in between my arm and my body. Caramel won't settle down until he's tried and failed, at least four or five times, to fall asleep right on my face. Shamrock always sleeps on the couch downstairs, no matter how many times I try to settle him on the bed with me, and Marigold has a spot under the window that she really likes, but sometimes she sleeps in her kennel instead, and I can never find Michelangelo in the morning and it always scares me, but he always turns up in my laundry basket or in the box with my tapes or under the bed, or sometimes he sneaks upstairs and sleeps with Todd, and the five others sleep all on top of each other in the corner on top of the extra comforter, but I checked all of those places this morning—every single one—and they're all gone, gone, gone.

Mom always tried to open windows because of the smell, but I'd stop her because I was afraid they would escape. Every day I breathe in feathers and dander and urine so they will not escape.

My mother sometimes curls her hand into a loose fist and presses her knuckles against my cheek. When she does, I smell her lotion, always lemongrass. Todd will do something similar, but it feels different, more urgent, when he does.

The animals. They were with me when I fell asleep last night. I didn't notice I was sleeping in my shoes, and I didn't notice when they left.

This is why I need more sleep. This is how things slip through my fingers.

My head is spinning with fourteen names I didn't protect.

"We'll find them, Craig," Mom says, with a hand on the back of my head. "They were probably just scared from the noise. They'll come back."

"They should have stayed in the basement," I whisper. "Why did they run away?"

Why were a few open doors enough incentive for them to leave?

I shouldn't have fallen asleep. I suck.

"We'll put up posters, Craig, okay?" Mom says. Like she doesn't have enough to worry about and people to call—insurance companies, someone to fix the window, and her mother to assure her that being this close to D.C. really doesn't mean we're going to die. It's been thirteen months, almost, since the terrorist attacks, and we're still convinced that any mishap means someone will steer a plane into one of our buildings.

We don't say that out loud.

Usually this time in the morning, I take all the different kinds of food and I fill all the bowls. They come running, tripping over themselves, rubbing against me, nipping my face and my hands like I am the food, like I just poured myself into a bowl and offered myself to them. Then I clean the litter boxes and the cages and take the dogs out for a walk.

I can do this all really, really quickly, after a year of practice.

Mom helps, usually, and sometimes I hear her counting under her breath, or staring at one of the animals, trying to figure out if one is new—sometimes yes, sometimes no.

The deal Mom and I have is no new animals. The deal is I don't have to give them away, I don't have to see a therapist, but I can't have any more animals. I don't want a therapist because therapists are stupid, and I am not crazy.

And the truth is it's not my fault. The animals find me. A kitten behind a Dumpster, a rabbit the girl at school can't keep. A dog too old for anyone to want. I just hope they find me again now that they're gone.

Part of the deal was also that Mom got to name a few of the newer ones, which is how I ended up with a few with really girly names.

But I love them. I tell them all the time. I'll pick Hail up and cuddle him to my face in that way that makes his ears get all twitchy. I'll make loose fists and hold them up to Marigold and Jupiter's cheeks. They'll lick my knuckles. "I love you," I tell them. It's always been really easy for me to say. I've never been one of those people who can't say it.

It's October 4th. Just starting to get cold, but it gets cold fast around here.

God, I hope they're okay.

I'm up way too early now that I don't have to feed the animals, but I don't know what else to do but get dressed and get ready for school. It takes like two minutes, and now what?

A year ago, back when it was still 2001 . . .
  Back when we still clung . . .
  Back when I slept upstairs . . .
  There was a boy.
  A very, very, very important boy.
  Now . . .
  There's Lio.
  Lio. I knew how it was spelled before I ever heard it out loud. It sounds normal, like Leo, but it looks so special. I love that.

I started talking to Lio back in June. I'm this thing for my school called an ambassador, which basically means I get good grades and I don't smoke, so they give out my email and a little bit about me to incoming students so I can gush about how cool this place is or something like that.

He sent me a message. He said he's about to move here, he's going to be at my school, we're the same age, and this is so creepy stalker, but you like Jefferson Airplane and I like Jefferson Airplane too, so cool, do you think we could IM sometime?

So he did and we are and I do and we did.

Lio is, to sum him up quickly, a koala. I realized that pretty early on.

He gets good grades, but he smokes, so he could never be an ambassador. There are a few reasons it's really, really stupid for Lio to smoke, but that doesn't seem to stop him. I don't know him well enough to admit that it scares me to death. And really, it seems like everything scares me to death now, so I've learned to shut up about it.

He's not a *boy* to me, not yet, because *boy* implies some kind of intimacy, but Lio is a boy in the natural sense of the word, at least I assume so, since I've never seen him with his clothes off and barely with his coat off, to be honest. Though I can imagine. And sometimes I do. Oh, God.

He wears a lot of hats. That's how we met for real, once his family moved here. I thought he'd come looking for me as soon as school started, but I couldn't find him anywhere, which was immediately a shame, because I was beginning to get sick of eating my lunch alone every day.

Then Ms. Hoole made both of us take our hats off in honors precalculus last month, on the third day of school.

"Lio, Craig," she said. "Your hats, present them here." And of course I didn't give a shit about my hat, because I had found Lio.

Lio didn't say anything, but his eyes said, *bitch,* and when he took his hat off I could see his hair was a chopped-up mess of four different colors, all of them muted and faded and fraying. Lio has a head like an old couch.

After class, he didn't go up to collect his hat, so I got both and brought his to him. He was rushing down the hallway, unlit cigarette between his fingers.

I said, "Lio?"

He looked at me and nodded.

I smiled a bit. "You weren't listening? I'm Craig."

He bit his bottom lip like he was trying not to laugh, but not in a bad way. In a really, really warm way, and I could tell because his eyes were locked onto mine.

There was a whole mess of people and he was still walking, but he kept looking at me.

"I like your hair," I told him, because it was difficult not to make some sort of comment.

Lio leaned against the wall and studied me. And even though I know now that Lio's really uncomfortable without a hat on, and he was really mad at Ms. Hoole for taking it and really mad at himself for being too afraid of talking to go up and ask for it back, he didn't pull the hat back on right away. He kept it crumpled up in his hand and he watched me instead.

And he covered his mouth a little and he smiled.

So here are some facts about Lio:

He has either five or six older sisters, I can't remember,

and one younger sister, and they are all very nice and love him a lot and call him nearly every day, except for his little sister, Michelle, and the youngest of the older sisters, Jasper, who are in middle school and high school, respectively, and therefore live with him and therefore only call him when he's in trouble or they want to borrow his clothes. I've only met Jasper. She is a senior, and much prettier than Lio. They all have cell phones, every single one of them, because they are from New York, and Lio says everyone has them there, and I don't know if that's true, but I'm really jealous.

He likes Colin Farrell, so when that movie *Phone Booth* comes out next month, we're going to go see it together. I don't know if this is a date or what, but I've already decided that I'm going to pay, and if he tries to protest I'm going to give him this smile and be like "No, no, let me."

He used to be a cancer kid—bald, skinny, mouth sores, leukemia. That was when he was five until he was seven, I think. He got to go to Alaska to see polar bears because of the Make-A-Wish Foundation. He said one time that the thing about cancer kids is no one knows what to do with them if they don't die. He's fine now, but he shouldn't be smoking cigarettes. He had a twin brother who died.

Today I come up to Lio's locker and he nods to me. The principal gave us American flags to put up on our lockers on September 11th, for the anniversary. Most of us put them up, but we also took them down again afterward, because they were cheap and flimsy and because it's been a year and patriotism is lame again. Lio still has his on his locker, but three weeks later it's started to fray. My father gave his school flags too. He's an elementary school principal. My mother is a social worker. My family is a little adorable.

Lio's flag flaps while he roots through his locker. He takes out a very small cage and hands it to me. I'm excited for a minute, thinking he's found one of the animals, maybe Peggy, the guinea pig. Even though there's no way she could fit in there, I'm still hoping, because maybe maybe maybe. But it's a small white mouse. Really, really pretty.

But it makes my head immediately list everyone that I've lost.

Four dogs: Jupiter, Casablanca, Kremlin, Marigold.

Five cats: Beaumont, Zebra, Shamrock, Sandwich, Caramel.

One bird: Fernando.

Three rabbits: Carolina, Hail, Michelangelo.

A guinea pig: Peggy.

"Made me think of you," he says, softly.

Because Lio says so few words, every single one has deep, metaphorical, cosmic significance in my life. And my words are like pennies.

I talk to the mouse very quietly on my way back to my

locker. I think I'll name her Zippers. I'm not sure why. I'm never sure why I choose the names I do. Maybe I should let Mom handle all of them, although she'd probably name this one Princess or something.

I should ask Lio what he'd like her to be named. Or where he got her. He doesn't know about the deal I have with my mom, and I feel no need to tell him.

I set her cage on top of my books.

Lio's there a minute later. He bites his thumbnail and fusses with his hat. His hair's still a mess, but it has nothing to do with the cancer. He's just sort of a psycho with his hair.

"My therapist says I'm a little fucked up," he explained to me one time, when I barely knew him, and that explanation terrified and intrigued me all at the same time. He sniffled and rubbed his nose. "Yeah."

Once I told him therapy is bullshit and he seemed offended, so I don't tell him that anymore, even though I still believe it.

"My animals are gone," I tell him now.

He looks up.

"Someone broke into my house last night. They broke the windows and left all the doors open, and all my animals left. They just ran out the doors or something . . ."

He watches me. Sometimes he does this, looks at me when I'm in the middle of talking, and it's like he's interrupting without saying a word, because I can't think with those eyes all blue on me. I can't think of anything else to say, and it makes me want to cry. Usually I can handle this, because I'm only talking about my brother or a class or my day. But right now it's a little more than I can stand.

I need Lio to say something.

But he doesn't. He reaches out and touches the tip of my finger with the tip of his finger.

Bing.

I swallow.

He says, "Did you look under the couch?"

Even stuff like that sounds profound from him, and I hate that all I can do is nod while I'm trying to get my voice back, because I always like to give Lio more of a response when he talks to me, since it's so hard to get words out of him.

"Yeah," I say eventually. "We looked under the couch."

"I'm sorry."

Lio's never seen my animals because he's never been to my house, but he's heard enough about them. Plus there are pictures of them all over my locker. I touch a Polaroid of Jemeena, this excellent hamster I had who died a few months ago. I couldn't bring myself to get any more hamsters after her.

I look at Lio.

I haven't been to Lio's place either. He says it's still full of boxes, because their apartment is so big that they don't even notice them taking up space. I think he's just used to his old tiny apartment in New York.

"I need to put up posters after school," I tell Lio. "Will you come help me?"

He nods.

"Thanks." The bell goes off and I close my locker door. "I hope they're still alive."

"It's not cold yet."

He probably wouldn't say that if he'd gone a whole night with wind pouring into his house. Getting out of the shower felt like a punishment. I say, "I know. They could probably have survived last night, I hope. What if maybe someone stole them off the street? I hope not." I breathe out.

He nods a little. "We'll find them."

We start walking to class, and this girl passing us waves to Lio, this tall blond girl with glasses and a pretty smile.

I say, "She'd be really hot if she were a boy."

Lio watches her go and nods slowly. I wish I knew what that meant. It would be something else to think about.

Todd is at my locker after second period. He substitute teaches here sometimes, so it's not that weird to see him, even though I didn't know he was working today. The substitute teaching thing isn't his real job. Really, he works nights at a suicide hotline, which pays even less than substitute

teaching. He's taking classes to get his masters in environ-
mental science. Then he's going to save us all before the
world explodes.

He holds up a paper bag. "You forgot your lunch."

This is why people need sleep. "Thanks," I say. I bet
Mom made him bring it to me. She's pretty intense about
lunch. She still packs mine every day, because she wants
me to get a lot of vitamins or whatever. I usually end up
giving half of it to Lio and eating chips instead. I'm not
going to tell Todd that.

"You doing okay?" he asks.

"What?"

He says, "Just checking in," and he gives me a hug with
one arm and then leaves. I open my lunch bag like I think
there's going to be some explanation of why he was so
affectionate, I guess because I wish it were something better
than *because he feels sorry for you and your lost animals.* But it's
just an apple and a sandwich and a bag of walnuts. I rip off
a bit of the apple for Zippers and stuff everything else into
my locker before I head off to my next class.

Lio is against the wall, standing with some girls that he
is half friends with. It's probably hard to be friends with a
kid that quiet, but I wouldn't know, because it's been very
easy for me to be whatever Lio and I are.

He smiles at me with the corner of his mouth when I
walk up. I give him the smallest little kick above his shoe.

"Has Lio been entertaining you with his witty banter?"
I ask.

The girls look uncomfortable, like they think maybe
I'm being mean. Lio looks away from me, but his smile is
a little bigger now. Heh. I couldn't even tell you what any
of these girls looks like, or whether I'd like any of them if
they were boys.

Silver Spring is a half city in the same way Lio is a half
koala. Lately they've been developing it more and more—
sticking in Whole Foods and rich hippie stuff like that, and
they started redoing the metro station so it's easier to get
downtown, which my parents say doesn't matter because
there's no way I'm riding the metro alone until I stop tripping over my feet and talking to strangers. But I guess it's
okay as long as I'm with Lio. I didn't ask.

We're at the Glenmont station now, me and Lio, to put
up signs. MANY MISSING PETS. DOGS, CATS, SMALL ANIMALS.
PLEASE CALL. REWARD.

FOUR DOGS

FIVE CATS

ONE BIRD

THREE RABBITS

A GUINEA PIG

I don't know what I'm going to do about a reward.
The mouse Lio gave me makes tiny chirping noises in my

backpack. I make sure she's safe in there, and she gets another bit of apple for being so good all day.

In the corner a man plays a harmonica, but he has an empty guitar case in front of him to collect money. He looks sort of like Lio—very small with big hands, a little grungy.

Lio isn't exactly grungy, but he's definitely more hardcore something than I am. At least, he's into ironic T-shirts—the one he's wearing now has a picture of a football with SOCCER over it—and jeans that sit too low on his hips. Usually black ones. I'm either preppier or lazier. I still wear the kind of clothes my mom said looked good on me when I was ten. Except I've grown nearly a foot since then, so I look older than fifteen, but I feel younger, and I think that's a big source of trouble for me.

It's five o'clock, and this is the last station we're covering today. Our hands are sore from stapling up posters, and we're still a little red because one of the guards at Shady Grove yelled at us and asked us if we had a permit or something. At every other station, we were left alone. It figures. I've never met a nice person at Shady Grove, ever.

We go up the escalator and into the outdoor area underneath the awning. "We could catch a bus," Lio says, though I don't know why, because I assume we're going to get on the metro and go back to Forest Glen, where I live, and he already said his dad would pick him up, no problem. I would be excited about the idea that he's coming home with me if it didn't mean that he was going to see my house without animals, so I made up some lie about how my parents don't let me invite friends in when they're not there so we'll just have to wait on the porch until his dad gets there, and I think maybe he knew I was lying and maybe he thinks I don't want him there. But it's just because of the animals. That's all it is.

It's just that I haven't invited anyone in for a really long time, I guess.

Anyway, there's no reason either of us should catch a bus.

Then he says, "We could get on a bus and go really far away."

I put my hand on his back. "Like New York?"

"Like outer space." He stiffens a little under my hand, so I take it away.

I try not to think about it, but I really don't know what I'm doing with Lio. I guess we're friends, sort of, except we don't really talk. We're the closest either one of us has to a friend, because I can't stand most people anymore and Lio left all the people who were used to him in New York, and it's pretty damn depressing until you consider that I really like being with Lio, and I hope he likes being with me. And we do spend a lot of time together. I don't know if Lio's into boys. It seems like a stupid question, because I don't know what difference the answer will make. The question isn't whether he's into boys. The question is if he's into me. I know lots of gay boys, after all—I'm in drama club—but here I am without a boyfriend.

It's starting to get dark. If the clocks had changed already, it would be Todd-coffee black out here by now. I guess we're lucky.

There are two guys, definitely older than us, slumming on the gate that separates the metro station from the church. Actually, they're not slumming. One of them is sitting on the gate and the other is swinging it back and forth, like he's rocking him to sleep. Except they're laughing.

A part of me loves Glenmont. I love the water tower here so much more than the one back at Forest Glen, which is short and fat and always looks like it's watching everything. Here, everything's dirty in a beautiful way. Grimy, I guess, is the word I'm looking for. Everything's covered and maybe protected by a layer of grime. I wish we went to school here instead of in Forest Glen, where all the houses and schools are tucked into little neighborhoods, like we have to hide. My school and my house are both in that one part of town, so it's like I can't ever get out of it.

"There's no way the animals would have gotten this far," I say. "They don't even know how to ride the metro. We should just go home and look there."

So we head back and get off the metro at Forest Glen and start walking toward my house. Todd's car is in the driveway. There goes my home-alone excuse.

"My brother can drive you home," I say.

He shakes his head. "Dad's coming at five fifteen."

"Oh."

"And it's, um, a little past five fifteen."

I guess that's good, because I don't think either he or Todd would really enjoy being stuck in a car together. Lio isn't known for responding well to normal social cues, never mind Todd's neurotic ones.

I guess I should invite Lio inside while we're waiting. That's not a big deal. It's just into the kitchen.

Lio says, "Craig."

I look up as he scurries under a bush and comes out with a little white kitten. Sandwich.

She's the newest of my animals. I was at the vet picking up antibiotics for Marigold, and she was there in a little box with four sisters, her eyes begging me, *hold me hold me hold me*, and I've never been able to resist that, ever, and now I take her from Lio and I have her. She's home. She didn't go far. She was just waiting for me.

She mews.

"Yours?" he asks.

I nod, because I'm not sure I can talk right now, or that I could say anything but Sandwich's name if I did. She's so dirty, and little bits of sticks cling to her. She looks up at me and mews again. I pet her cheek with my thumb, and then I give Lio a big smile.

He strokes her head for a minute, then says to me, very quietly, "Happy?"

I nod.

He leans in and kisses me.

It's soft and small. It's 5:20 p.m.

My parents decide we need to have BLTs with our pork chops in honor of Sandwich's return. It's weird, because we usually eat in front of the TV, but now we're all sitting at the table together, and it's so quiet without the news in the background or the animals underfoot.

Sandwich paws at my shoelace.

My father has this way of chewing that makes it look like a job. It's like he's considering every muscle in his jaw every time he uses it, like he's constantly reevaluating to make sure he's working at the right pace and pressure. When he was sixteen—only a year older than me, but when I imagine it he always looks twenty-five—he was a big-shot football player who got sidelined with a major head injury and had to do rehab and staples in his head and all of it. He and Lio should start a club of people who shouldn't be alive, and Mom and I can start a club of people who shouldn't be jealous but are, a little, because we will never really understand. My ex-boyfriend could be in that second club too. Or maybe he's my boyfriend. This isn't the kind of thing I want to think about.

Anyway, Dad says he recovered all the way, and Mom didn't meet him until years afterward, so we have to take his word for it, but whenever he does something weird like chew like a trash compactor or leave his keys in the refrigerator, I always picture these football-shaped neurons on his head struggling to connect to each other.

I can't believe Lio kissed me. Well, I can, but I think it's weird that he asked me "Happy?" first. If I had said no, would he have kissed me? Was it a reward for being happy, the same way I reward him when he talks? Was he thanking me for being happy?

It's been ten months since my last kiss. I don't know how long it's been since I've really been happy, but ten months is a good guess.

Todd rubs the skin between his eyes. I think his head is still bothering him.

Mom didn't have any luck finding the animals, but we're going to go back out tonight after dinner and keep looking. Mom says if Sandwich was out there, safe, the others must be too.

Dad says, "It's probably for the best."

I frown.

He says, "This isn't a barn, Craig. Maybe now you'll get out of the house, hmm? Start going out with your friends again."

"I don't have any friends."

"Are there any nice boys at school?" he says, in that way, and I guess I should be thankful that he says this no differently from how he asks Todd about girls at work, but I'm not, I just want him to pretend I'm a eunuch or something, especially since I pretty much am at this point, anyway.

Mom gives him a stern look. "We'll find them." She looks at me. "You know, your friend could have stayed for dinner." Now she's totally giving me a chance to tell her that Lio's more than a friend, and I have no idea what to say. The fact that my parents are entirely okay with my homosexuality makes talking about it kind of difficult, because when you're gay and single the only thing you have going for you is imagined shock value. The reality is that it's pretty boring to be like, *hey, parents, I'm gay, and there's absolutely no reason for you to give a shit right now.*

So I just say, "That's okay," and concentrate on cutting my pork chop.

And to be honest, calling Lio my friend seems wrong, probably because I don't remember, really, how to have friends. That sounds so pathetic, because I used to have friends, but then I had a boyfriend and sort of ignored everybody, and then after the boyfriend exploded I stopped being fun and started blowing people off when they asked me to hang out. It's not like everyone hates me, and I have people to talk to in classes but not once we're out in the halls, those sorts of friends. And I spend a lot of evenings here with the animals, and they were enough, in a way my parents could never appreciate and could barely tolerate.

Now what? Now I don't know, I guess maybe Lio's my new animal. And Sandwich, of course. And Zipper. I should make a picture book about us or something. Two teenage boys and two animals—this is the 2002 version of the blended family.

I can't believe I'm thinking of him as a familial candidate. I mean, come on, I barely know the kid. What do we even do together? Sometimes we go skateboarding because, I don't know, I guess we think we're eleven. He smokes clove cigarettes and I pretend I don't hate the smell. We drink Slurpees and . . . we do stuff like push each other on gates, I guess.

I wish I knew what was going on.

I really can't get into this right now. I probably shouldn't have kissed him back. But I've sort of wanted to kiss him ever since I saw his fucked-up hair that day in Ms. Hoole's class, and really since the conversation right after, when he told me he cuts it when he's nervous, and I immediately wanted to know everything in the whole world that makes him nervous, and everything in the whole world about him.

I should have invited him to stay tonight. He'd fit well into this silence at the dinner table. I think it's bad when I'm allowed to dwell in my head for this long. Someone should be dragging me out into conversation, but usually it's someone on TV and tonight there's no TV.

It's not that we don't get along—my parents and my brother and me—it's that we don't have a whole lot in common, and we all have these different ideas of how to use this house and this family. My dad wants a house full of books and rousing dinner-table discussions about whether or not Lolita was a slut. My mom is already talking about arranging a Secret Santa thing among the four of us, won't that be fun? My brother wants this to be his airport, his temporary base in all his running around, complete with full-service restaurant and four-dollar massages, and he'll pay for us by the hour, no problem, if we will just treat him as well as he deserves. But we never do, even I know that.

And I want something to take care of.

We listen to Dad squeak his knife around for a minute. It's brutal. Todd clears his throat, then he stands up and turns on the radio. He plunks it down in the center of the table like it's something for us to eat.

My father sighs, a little.

Todd tunes the radio to a news station and settles back into his green beans. The radio switches from weather to local news. A few car accidents, a stabbing, and two shootings, both in Glenmont. One was through the window of this craft store, Michael's, about a quarter mile from the

Glenmont metro. The bullet didn't hit anyone. An hour later and two miles away, a bullet did—someone in the parking lot of the Shopper's Food Warehouse. He's dead.

My father shakes his head while he drinks.

"Weird it made the news," Todd said. "People get shot all the time."

My father says, "Not while they're shopping," which is pretty representative of his world view. My dad's old enough that even September 11th didn't change his mind that violence only happens to violent people. The only people who get stabbed are in gangs. The only people who get shot, shot someone else first. As much as my bleeding heart wants to convince him this is wrong, the truth is most of the violence here *is* revenge-driven or gang-related. I should know, I mean, I go to public school.

The first shooting was at 5:20. That was when Lio kissed me, that was the exact minute. I know because I checked my watch afterward because I wanted to see how long it lasted, then I realized I hadn't checked my watch before he kissed me, so I'd never know. But I don't think it was very long, really.

No one died in the 5:20 shooting, which would have been kind of crazy romantic in this horrible way, and it would have given me an excuse to call him. But I don't think he would like the symbolism of "so, we're just a like a bullet that didn't hit anybody" any more than I do.

God, I hope he wouldn't like it any more than I do.

My mom finishes her dinner and stands up. "Ready, Craig?"

I say "Yeah," and pull on my jacket. I hope I don't get shot. That's pretty weird. I've never thought anything like that before. That kiss has me all screwed up.

We swing our flashlights back and forth, whistling and calling out names. Mom checks behind bushes and under the railing of the walkway to the metro. There's a couple making out on the bridge above us. I think it's one boy and one girl. Todd swears that he saw two homeless people having sex up there once—one boy and one girl.

"There are a lot of frogs here," I say. "We could get a frog."

She laughs in this way that says she doesn't know if I'm kidding.

"I only go for the fuzzy ones," I tell her.

"All right."

I take my comment out of context in my head and giggle a little. I only go for the fuzzy ones. Heh. This is a gross thing to be laughing about in front of your mom.

She's wearing the brown patchwork jacket I got her a million Christmases ago. She blows on her hands and runs them through her hair. "I hope we find Casablanca," she says. "She's my favorite." Casablanca is a Labrador retriever. She's old and missing a leg.

"We'll find her," I say. "She's easy. Easy to describe in posters and stuff. Easy to hear coming."

But the cold is making my nose run and making it a little hard to breathe, and right now nothing sounds very easy.

I wipe my nose.

Mom flicks her flashlight beam to me, and I look away quickly. "It's cold," I say stupidly, and crunch some of the leaves on the ground. It's not like she'd get upset if I were crying. I cry like three times a day, so it's the opposite of a big deal. It'd be like getting concerned every time I eat a meal.

Mom says, "I called the shelter this morning. They have all their descriptions, and they're all looking out, just waiting for someone to bring them in."

"Okay."

She says, "I'm so sorry this happened, sweetheart."

"We're going to find them. We're going to find all of them. That's right, yeah?"

"Yes." Mom cups her hand around the back of my head. "That's right."

I felt better when Lio comforted me, but it's still nice to be here for a minute, with Mom, searching for animals that she never even wanted.

We find Jupiter, who's this amazing Chihuahua-pug mix, trying to pick a fight with some bigger dogs a few blocks away. We start to head home with him, and my heart is pounding against his little body, and then we find Caramel, and just when everything feels so, so amazing, we find my parakeet, Fernando, except he's dead.

It's like a punch in the chest.

But Caramel and Jupiter scurry out of my arms as soon as we're home and go rub up against the couch and chew on the rug, and everything feels a little more possible again.

I leave them for a minute to go outside. I make a cross out of sticks and scratch Fernando's name in the dirt, then I cross it out and write Flamingo instead. He would have liked that.

But he isn't buried here. I didn't move his body from where we found it by the side of the road. I was too scared. I didn't want to touch it. I suck.

We're still missing:

Three dogs.

Three cats.

Three rabbits.

A guinea pig.

I close my eyes and listen to the animals inside my head and the memory of his chirping and the silence all the way around me.